A NEW HOME

(INN BY THE SEA—BOOK 3)

FIONA GRACE

Fiona Grace

Fiona Grace is author of the LACEY DOYLE COZY MYSTERY series, comprising nine books; of the TUSCAN VINEYARD COZY MYSTERY series, comprising seven books; of the DUBIOUS WITCH COZY MYSTERY series, comprising three books; of the BEACHFRONT BAKERY COZY MYSTERY series, comprising six books; of the CATS AND DOGS COZY MYSTERY series, comprising nine books; of the ELIZA MONTAGU COZY MYSTERY series, comprising nine books (and counting); of the ENDLESS HARBOR ROMANTIC COMEDY series, comprising nine books (and counting); of the INN AT DUNE ISLAND ROMANTIC COMEDY series, comprising five books (and counting); of the INN BY THE SEA ROMANTIC COMEDY series, comprising five books (and counting); and of the MAID AND THE MANSION COZY MYSTERY series, comprising five books (and counting).

Fiona would love to hear from you, so please visit www.fionagraceauthor.com to receive free ebooks, hear the latest news, and stay in touch.

MURDER AT THE HEDGEROW (Book #1)
A DALLOP OF DEATH (Book #2)
CALAMITY AT THE BALL (Book #3)
A SPEAKEASY DEMISE (Book #4)
A FLAPPER FATALITY (Book #5)
BUMPED BY A DAME (Book #6)
A DOLL'S DEBACLE (Book #7)
A FELLA'S RUIN (Book #8)
A GAL'S OFFING (Book #9)

LACEY DOYLE COZY MYSTERY
MURDER IN THE MANOR (Book#1)
DEATH AND A DOG (Book #2)
CRIME IN THE CAFE (Book #3)
VEXED ON A VISIT (Book #4)
KILLED WITH A KISS (Book #5)
PERISHED BY A PAINTING (Book #6)
SILENCED BY A SPELL (Book #7)
FRAMED BY A FORGERY (Book #8)
CATASTROPHE IN A CLOISTER (Book #9)

TUSCAN VINEYARD COZY MYSTERY
AGED FOR MURDER (Book #1)
AGED FOR DEATH (Book #2)
AGED FOR MAYHEM (Book #3)
AGED FOR SEDUCTION (Book #4)
AGED FOR VENGEANCE (Book #5)
AGED FOR ACRIMONY (Book #6)
AGED FOR MALICE (Book #7)

DUBIOUS WITCH COZY MYSTERY
SKEPTIC IN SALEM: AN EPISODE OF MURDER (Book #1)
SKEPTIC IN SALEM: AN EPISODE OF CRIME (Book #2)
SKEPTIC IN SALEM: AN EPISODE OF DEATH (Book #3)

BEACHFRONT BAKERY COZY MYSTERY
BEACHFRONT BAKERY: A KILLER CUPCAKE (Book #1)
BEACHFRONT BAKERY: A MURDEROUS MACARON (Book #2)

BEACHFRONT BAKERY: A PERILOUS CAKE POP (Book #3)
BEACHFRONT BAKERY: A DEADLY DANISH (Book #4)
BEACHFRONT BAKERY: A TREACHEROUS TART (Book #5)
BEACHFRONT BAKERY: A CALAMITOUS COOKIE (Book #6)

CATS AND DOGS COZY MYSTERY
A VILLA IN SICILY: OLIVE OIL AND MURDER (Book #1)
A VILLA IN SICILY: FIGS AND A CADAVER (Book #2)
A VILLA IN SICILY: VINO AND DEATH (Book #3)
A VILLA IN SICILY: CAPERS AND CALAMITY (Book #4)
A VILLA IN SICILY: ORANGE GROVES AND VENGEANCE (Book #5)
A VILLA IN SICILY: CANNOLI AND A CASUALTY (Book #6)

CHAPTER ONE

Chesham Cove, England, glittered in the fading dusk light as Charlotte Moore stared out her bedroom window. The quaint village sprawled at the edge of a calm sea, looking like something out of a fairytale as the horizon turned into an alchemy of amber and sapphire. The gentle summer evening breeze, infused with the briny scent of the ocean, rustled through the nearby cliffs where wildflowers clung to their rugged edges and right into Charlotte's open window. It was a summer evening that seemed to whisper promises, and Charlotte felt excited by the evening's possibilities.

Inside The Old Crown Inn, Charlotte turned to the antique mirror that hung in her private quarters, her reflection caught within the intricate details of the frame. She nervously adjusted her outfit, smoothing out the wrinkles on her delicate sundress and twirling a strand of chestnut hair around her finger. Simon would be here any minute, and Charlotte was giddy with excitement. She looked forward to spending the evening with him—the latest in what was getting to be several months of dating.

"Come on, Charlotte, no reason to be nervous," she whispered to herself, taking a deep breath and straightening her posture. She wanted to make a good impression on Simon, to show him that she was ready for a new beginning after the all-too-recent tumultuous end to her marriage. Charlotte was grateful for the opportunity to start anew with someone who seemed to understand her in a way that no one else had for a very long time. She hadn't expected to fall for someone so soon after her impromptu move to England, but she wasn't going to let the wounds of her old marriage hold her back from the fun she'd been having with Simon. Her ex, Daniel, had been the one to choose the split—and now, she was choosing. Her new business, her new love, and a new start.

As she made her way down the stairs of the inn, the smell of dinner wafted through the air. In the cozy kitchen of The Old Crown Inn, Charlotte had been busy preparing a classic British meal. The

1

centerpiece of the dinner was a beautifully roasted beef Wellington, its golden, flaky pastry crust encasing a tender, perfectly cooked fillet of beef. Alongside it, she had prepared a rich, velvety red wine jus, its savory aroma mingling with the scent of the roast.

For the sides, Charlotte had chosen honey-roasted carrots and parsnips, their edges caramelized to a sweet perfection, and a dish of steamed green beans, bright and crisp. A creamy, indulgent cauliflower cheese, bubbling with a golden crust, sat waiting to be served.

The table was set with vintage China—a gift that the attic of The Crown had yielded on a slightly terrifying venture into the upper recesses of the old house— each plate adorned with a sprig of fresh rosemary from the garden. In the center of the table, a simple but elegant arrangement of wildflowers, picked from the cliffs, added a touch of color. She took a moment to appreciate the scene, feeling a sense of pride and anticipation for the evening ahead. Soon, Simon would arrive, and they would share this special meal together.

The moment Charlotte had been anticipating finally arrived as the sound of the door knocker echoed through the quiet inn. Her heart fluttered with excitement; this was it, Simon was here. She hurried to the door, her steps light on the old wooden floors, each creak a familiar note in the symphony of The Old Crown Inn's history.

Opening the door, Charlotte was greeted by the sight of Simon, standing in the soft glow of the porch light. He looked every bit the gentleman, his attire smart yet casual, perfectly suited for the evening. In his hand, he held a bouquet of flowers, their colors vibrant against the twilight backdrop. The bouquet was a beautiful mix of wildflowers, reminiscent of those she had picked for the dinner table, each petal seemingly capturing the essence of the summer evening.

Charlotte's face lit up with a radiant smile, her eyes sparkling with delight. "Simon, they're beautiful," she exclaimed, admiring the flowers. There was an ease in her voice, a warmth that spoke of comfort and familiarity—and happiness. It wasn't lost on Charlotte that she hadn't heard her own voice sound like that in many years. Simon returned her smile, his own eyes reflecting joy.

"Only the best for you, love," Simon replied, handing her the bouquet. "They reminded me of this place, of you. And you look beautiful," he said, his eyes sparkling with admiration.

"Thank you," Charlotte replied, feeling a blush creeping into her cheeks. There was an awkwardness to their interaction, but she relished the newness of it.

As she took the flowers, their hands brushed lightly, sending a ripple of excitement through her. Charlotte invited Simon in, leading him through the dimly lit corridors of the inn, their footsteps a soft patter against the hush of the evening. Reaching the dining room, Charlotte showed Simon the table she had meticulously prepared. Simon's eyes took in the scene with an appreciative gaze.

"This looks incredible, Charlotte," he said, admiration evident in his tone. "You've outdone yourself."

"Please, let's sit. Everything's ready."

As they sat down for dinner, Charlotte and Simon made small talk, and she smiled at the way his eyes lit up as he spoke. They ate and laughed and leaned close to one another, their hands brushing against each other's, and Charlotte felt a nervous energy buzzing within her, hyperaware of Simon's presence beside her. Taking a bite of her food, she snuck a glance at his rugged profile, taking in the way the soft kitchen light accentuated his handsome features.

"This is fantastic," Simon said, breaking the silence between them. "If owning a B&B doesn't work out, you could always be a chef."

Charlotte nodded, laughing, tucking a strand of windswept hair behind her ear. "I bet I would fare a lot better as a chef here than back home in New York," she replied softly. "The culinary world there is very cutthroat."

"I prefer you here, anyway," Simon said, smiling. Then, Simon stopped, turning to face Charlotte. Her nervous energy intensified as he reached for her hand, his rough, calloused fingers intertwining with her slender ones.

"I'm glad you *found* your way here," he murmured, his sky-blue eyes boring into hers. Charlotte's heart quickened, a blush rising to her cheeks. She wondered if he could hear it thudding in her chest.

The moment stretched between them, weighted with anticipation. Charlotte wet her lips, torn between wanting to stay in this perfect moment and yearning to close the space between them. Before she could decide, Simon leaned in, his hand coming up to cradle her cheek. Charlotte's eyes fluttered shut as his lips met hers in a soft, tentative kiss. Warmth flooded through her and she sighed into the kiss. After a moment, Charlotte pulled back slowly, her eyes opening to meet Simon's tender gaze. She drew in a shaky breath, her heart racing.

"Wow," Simon whispered, a smile tugging at his lips.

Charlotte let out a soft laugh. "Wow is right."

Simon brushed his thumb over her cheekbone, his expression turning serious. "Charlotte, I-"

"Mom!"

They sprang apart as Amelia came bounding into the kitchen, her face alight with excitement.

"Amelia!" Charlotte pressed a hand to her fluttering heart. "You're home early. I thought you were meeting someone for coffee."

"I wanted to see you before your big date." Amelia hustled over to throw her arms around Charlotte in an exuberant hug before turning to Simon with a bright smile. "Hi Simon! It's so nice to see you again."

Simon chuckled, returning the smile. "You too, Amelia. How's summer break going?"

As Amelia launched into a detailed account of her adventures in Chesham Cove since her arrival, Charlotte observed the easy rapport between them, her heart swelling. Simon listened attentively, interjecting an occasional question or funny remark that made Amelia giggle. It had been ages since Charlotte had heard her college-aged, all-grown-up daughter giggle. This was the Amelia she remembered from easier days - playful, enthusiastic, fully present. Charlotte realized that Simon's warm, gentle spirit had likely played a role in coaxing out this lighter side of her daughter again. Charlotte felt a sense of rightness. Here, in this seaside village, with her daughter thriving and a man who saw past her faults to the goodness within, she had found a new beginning.

Watching them, Charlotte felt a sense of peace settles over her. She smiled as she watched Amelia and Simon chat, though her mind was still reeling from their kiss. She couldn't remember the last time she had felt such an instant connection with someone.

"Oh, I almost forgot!" Amelia suddenly exclaimed, turning to Charlotte. "Happy 4th of July!"

Charlotte blinked in surprise. "Is it the 4th already?"

"Yep! Independence Day!" Amelia gave an exaggerated wink.

"Too bad they don't celebrate it here, huh?" Simon said, sounding a bit sad.

"Darn British," Charlotte joked. She tapped her chin thoughtfully. "Well, I suppose we'll just have to have our own little Independence Day party. What do you say?"

"Yes!" Amelia clapped excitedly. "We need flags, and fireworks, and apple pie!"

"And we could have a barbecue on the beach!" Simon added with a grin.

Charlotte laughed. "I don't think we'll be able to get fireworks on such short notice. But I'm sure we can scrounge up some red, white and blue decorations from the inn's storage."

"Oooh, we could make s'mores over the barbecue!" Amelia said. "I'll see if I can find sparklers or poppers or something for makeshift fireworks. But later. I just came to make sure you crazy kids were behaving." Another wink had Charlotte blushing.

"Amelia! Really?"

"Gotta go, coffee waits!"

As Amelia dashed off, Charlotte met Simon's warm gaze. "Thanks for being so great with her," she said softly.

Simon squeezed her hand. "Of course. She's a terrific kid."

Charlotte nodded, her heart full. "She really is."

They resumed their dinner, the interruption having added a layer of comfortable ease to their evening. Charlotte savored each bite, her taste buds delighting in the flavors of the meal she had prepared. The conversation flowed naturally, a gentle current of shared interests and laughter—and, a little disappointingly, no more kisses.

As they finished their meal, Charlotte's thoughts drifted to the next several days. She had planned a few house projects to tackle with Amelia, a way to spend quality time with her daughter and keep restoring The Old Crown Inn in to a charming, pristine condition. There was also the excitement of new guests checking in, a family from America, bringing with them a slice of the home she had left behind. Charlotte looked forward to welcoming them, sharing stories, and perhaps introducing them to the magic of Chesham Cove.

"I've got a busy few days," Charlotte said, collecting the dishes. "Sightseeing with Amelia, and the day after, reno, new guests…"

Simon helped her with the dishes, his presence a comforting rhythm in the quiet kitchen. "Need any help with the projects?"

Charlotte smiled at his offer. "I think we've got it, but thank you. It's nice, having Amelia here for the summer. We're making the most of it. And she is getting a kick out of playing hostess at the inn. It's great having a second set of hands for when I have to be out of the house."

"I can see that," Simon said, a softness in his voice. "It's good to see you both so happy."

As they finished cleaning up, the last of the evening light faded, giving way to a blanket of stars. Simon walked Charlotte to the door, their hands lingering in a gentle goodbye.

"I had a wonderful evening, Charlotte. Thank you for dinner," Simon said, his eyes holding hers.

"Me too, Simon. Thank you for coming." She stood on her tiptoes, giving him a quick, tender kiss on the cheek. With a final wave, Simon left, and Charlotte closed the door, leaning against it for a moment. She felt a sense of contentment, a lightness in her heart. Tomorrow would be a new day at The Old Crown Inn, and so would the days after, filled with the laughter of her daughter, the arrival of new faces, and the continuation of her own journey in Chesham Cove. She looked forward to it all.

CHAPTER TWO

The Crown Inn and its inhabitants awoke to the harmonious cacophony of seagulls, their calls a reminder of the vast ocean just a stone's throw away. The air was rich with saline whispers, carrying with it the briny promise of the sea. Below the chorus of the seabirds, a gentle breeze danced through the leaves of the sentinel trees that stood guard around the perimeter of the inn, their branches swaying in a rhythmic ballet.

There was just something about this place—this little town—that made Charlotte feel *poetic.*

Inside, the dining area exuded a warmth that seemed to hum from the very grain of the polished wood table and kitchen countertops. Charlotte found a comforting solitude in her morning ritual. The aroma of fresh baking wafted through the room, mingling with the earthy scent of steeped tea leaves that lingered like an old friend.

"Can you believe this place doesn't do bagels?" Amelia said with mock indignation, a playful light dancing in her eyes as she spread a generous layer of clotted cream onto her scone, each movement precise and ladylike – a far cry from the boisterous child who used to smear jam over her cheeks with glee.

"Blasphemy," Charlotte replied, matching her daughter's tone while hiding her amusement behind a sip of Earl Grey. She watched Amelia, her heart swelling with pride. Her daughter was a woman, no longer a little girl—and Charlotte wondered how that had happened so fast.

"Seriously though, Mom, these scones are incredible," Amelia continued, pausing to take a bite. Her eyes closed in appreciation, a contented sigh escaping her lips.

"Maybe we can add them to our 'Things New York Could Learn from Chesham Cove' list," Charlotte suggested, the corners of her mouth curving into a smile.

"Right after 'How to Properly Queue'," Amelia quipped, and they both broke into laughter, the sound filling the space between them.

Charlotte leaned back in her dining chair, watching Amelia with a fondness that ached sweetly in her chest. When Amelia laughed, she looked so much like her father—and Charlotte was at once both troubled and sweetly nostalgic at the thought of her ex-husband, Daniel. They'd finally settled their divorce after he'd shown up here in England to make a poorly contrived bid to win her back—as though the split had been her idea! But nothing had changed, and the thought of going back to the emotional prison of her old life had been anathema to Charlotte. So, papers signed, Daniel sent packing back to New York, here she was—free.

The Crown this morning was a place where the weight of change felt a *little* less heavy. Despite the divorce, Charlotte felt she could still appreciate what she'd had without harboring regrets. After all, her marriage had given her Amelia.

"Your laughter is the best sound this old inn has heard in years," Charlotte remarked, her voice threaded with sincerity.

"Only because I get it from you," Amelia replied, reaching across the table to give her mother's hand a gentle squeeze.

For a moment, they sat in comfortable silence, each lost in their thoughts, the serenity of The Crown wrapping around them like a warm embrace. Charlotte pondered the journey that had led them here to this unexpected chapter of their lives. It was a time for healing, not just for the inn with its newly adorned walls and rejuvenated gardens, but for her own bruised heart.

"Remember when you insisted on eating breakfast for a whole month wearing your princess tiara?" Charlotte mused, her eyes crinkling at the corners as she sipped her tea. The memory was vivid, a picture painted in the hues of yesteryear, where their dining room had been a kingdom for weeks.

Amelia chuckled, setting down her scone. "And you played along, donning that ridiculous jester hat. Dad almost spit out his coffee when he saw us."

Charlotte's smile faltered for a moment, the second thought of Daniel a ghost passing through the conversation. But she quickly recovered. *Appreciate. Don't regret.*

"You've grown up so much since then." Her voice was soft.

"Seems like a lifetime ago," Amelia said, reaching again for her mother's hand, an anchor of warmth.

"Maybe a few," Charlotte agreed, squeezing back. She traced a finger along the rim of her porcelain teacup, the delicate China pattern echoing the intricate latticework of her thoughts. The inn's dining area, with its warm wooden floors and the scent of fresh scones wafting through the air, seemed an intimate stage for confessions.

"Amelia," Charlotte began, her voice hesitant as she set down her cup with a soft clink. "I've been thinking..."

"About?" Amelia prompted, her smile fading into a look of attentive concern.

"Us," Charlotte admitted, feeling the weight of vulnerability tighten around her chest. "Our relationship... Now that you're grown, it's changing, evolving. But I don't want to lose what we have." She picked at the frayed edge of the tablecloth, avoiding her daughter's steady gaze.

Amelia smiled softly. "Mom, we're not losing anything. We're just adding more layers to it, like this inn." Her thumb gently stroked Charlotte's knuckles. "You're creating something beautiful here, something lasting. Our relationship is the same. It's growing, adapting."

"I know," Charlotte sighed, the warmth from Amelia's touch seeping into her bones. "But the fear is still there. You're growing up, finding your own path, and I'm..." She paused, searching for the words. "I'm rediscovering who I am too. I don't want us to drift apart in the process. Your father and I—he said that we had grown apart, and I just—"

"Hey," Amelia said softly, squeezing her mother's hand a little tighter. "We're in this together, remember? Nothing could pull us apart—only bring us closer in ways we don't expect. I'm grateful for this chance to be friends, not just mother and daughter."

Charlotte met Amelia's earnest eyes, and in them, she saw a reflection of her own resolve. "Friends..." She let the word roll around her tongue, tasting its sweet potential.

"Exactly," Amelia affirmed, releasing Charlotte's hand to gesture expansively around the room. "And friends make new memories, right? So let's make some."

A smile tugged at the corners of Charlotte's lips as she absorbed Amelia's words.

Amelia's eyes sparkled with enthusiasm. "This is my first time in Chesham Cove, after all. We should explore every nook and cranny."

"Starting with the local shops?" Charlotte proposed, already picturing the antique stores and boutiques lining the cobbled streets.

"Then a walk on the beach?" Amelia leaned forward, the seaside luring her with its eternal call. "I can't get enough of the sand between my toes. The beach here is nothing like in New York."

"Sounds perfect," Charlotte affirmed, her heart swelling at the thought of spending the day alongside her daughter.

They rose from the table, the chairs scraping softly against the wooden floor, their movements harmonized in a shared rhythm. As they gathered their belongings, Charlotte tucked away the tendrils of nostalgia—and any pangs of pain—letting the anticipation of the day's adventures wash over her.

"Let's not forget to take a look at the bookshop by the pier," Charlotte reminded, as they made their way toward the door. "They have a wonderful selection of poetry."

"Maybe I'll find something for the plane ride home," Amelia said, opening the door for her mother. They stepped out onto the porch, greeted by the salty tang of sea air mingling with the earthy scent of the nearby trees.

Charlotte hesitated on the threshold, her nose wrinkling at the mention of Amelia going back to The States. The summer couldn't last forever, but Charlotte could at least ignore that it would end, for now. Fall semester would encroach soon enough.

Her gaze swept across The Crown's transformed facade. The once-dilapidated walls now boasted a fresh coat of paint, a soft cream that seemed to have absorbed the calmness of the sea itself. The new porch furniture, arranged thoughtfully. A splash of color caught her eye, and she smiled at the vibrant flowers blooming with abandon, their petals a kaleidoscope against the inn's renewed exterior.

"Look at this place, Mom," Amelia said, her voice laced with pride. "You've really turned it into something special."

"We're not done yet, darling," Charlotte replied, her satisfaction evident as she admired the fruits of her labor. "But it feels like a different world from when we first arrived."

Charlotte allowed herself a final glance back at The Crown, and then, with a deep breath, she turned toward the promise of the day, Amelia by her side, and together they ventured toward the quaint heart of Chesham Cove. Together, they strolled along the stone path weaving through the garden, the crunch of gravel underfoot punctuating their silent reverie. Her thoughts wandered, almost helplessly, to thoughts of Daniel. It was hard not to think of him with Amelia here.

"Mom?" Amelia's gentle inquiry drew Charlotte back from her introspection. "Are you okay?"

"Of course," Charlotte responded, her smile returning as she met Amelia's concerned gaze. "Just thinking about house stuff."

Amelia nodded, seemingly understanding the unspoken in her mother's words. They continued their walk, and Charlotte's heels clicked against the cobblestones, a rhythmic accompaniment to the cheerful buzz of Chesham Cove's morning. Shops with awnings in hues of ocean blue and sandy beige unfurled like petals, greeting the day alongside the women. The scents of salt and blooming hydrangeas mingled together, wrapping around Charlotte and Amelia as they meandered through the streets, laughter spilling from them.

"You used to *pursue* the pigeons down at Central Park," Charlotte teased, her voice laced with warmth.

Amelia chuckled, shoulders shaking with the memory. "I was convinced they had a secret pigeon society. And I wanted in."

"Seems you've always been an adventurer," Charlotte replied, squeezing her daughter's hand. They both knew the paths they walked now were far different from those childhood chases—and Charlotte leaned on Amelia's reassurances that their new paths would always intertwine.

Their stroll led them past quaint storefronts until they came upon a bookstore nestled between a bakery and a florist near the pier. Its windows displayed stacks of well-loved novels and new releases begging to be explored. With a shared glance, they entered, a bell tinkling above the door announcing their arrival.

"Smells like history and dreams in here," Amelia mused, taking a deep breath.

"Bound up in leather and paper," Charlotte added, trailing her fingers across the spines of books that lined the shelves. They lost themselves among the rows, each title a whisper of another world. Then, Amelia pulled out a slim volume, its cover worn.

"Look, Mom, it's that poetry book you used to read to me when I was little."

"Ah, yes." Charlotte took the book, flipping it open to a dog-eared page. "I told you the selection here was great. This one might have traveled far," she added, pointing to a stamp in the front of the book that said "Los Angeles Public Library."

"Speaking of going far...I know Dad's decision hit you hard," Amelia said, the playfulness in her tone giving way to gentle seriousness. Charlotte felt the weight of her daughter's gaze, earnest and searching. "Were you thinking of him when we left the house? Does it bother you, remind you, since I'm here?"

"Life throws us curveballs, doesn't it?" Charlotte whispered, her eyes locked on the faded print, not really seeing the words. "Yes, I was thinking abut your dad. About how we failed. But I am nothing but overjoyed that you came to England."

"Mom," Amelia began, hesitantly, "you're more than just Dad's ex-wife. You're this incredible, strong woman who started over in a new country, who's making The Crown into something beautiful."

"Amelia, I—"

"Let me finish," Amelia interjected softly. "We might not be the family we once were, but we're still a family. And I support you, no matter what."

Charlotte closed the book, setting it back on the shelf, and enveloped Amelia in a tight embrace. "My sweet girl, your faith in me is my greatest strength."

"Always," Amelia whispered, echoing the promise from before.

With the bookstore behind them, they continued on, finding their way to a local art gallery. The hushed space was filled with canvases splashed with color and sculptures that seemed to pulse with life. Charlotte's artistic soul ignited as she surveyed the pieces, each brushstroke a record of someone else's vision.

"Your work should be up here too, Mom," Amelia said, admiration evident in her voice.

"Maybe one day," Charlotte responded, allowing herself a moment to dream of such a future. But for now, she savored the present. Moving to Chesham had reignited her passion for painting, but she still struggled with the artistic rejection she'd felt back in The States— Daniel's sour stance on her art, the rejection of galleries. She just wanted to enjoy her newly rediscovered zest for the arts without pressure.

The day was waning as Charlotte and Amelia made their way back to The Crown, the coastal air now carrying a hint of evening's coming chill. Arms full of packages wrapped in brown paper and twine, they navigated the cobbled street with an easy grace that spoke of contented exhaustion. Each parcel held a bit of the day's discoveries – books that smelled of must and mystery, delicate seashells from the beach souvenir shop, and handmade scarves and other trinkets from the town's artisans.

"Look at us," Amelia chuckled, balancing a precarious stack of packages as she unlocked the door. "We could open our own little shop with all these finds."

"Or at least host one grand party," Charlotte replied, her eyes crinkling with mirth.

Stepping through the weathered door of The Crown, there was an audible exhale, a mutual release of breath that seemed to acknowledge the relief of returning. The inn enveloped them in a familiar embrace. A quick glance at the website admin page on the reception desk laptop revealed a new entry – a booking for the suite overlooking the garden in a few weeks, guests surely drawn by the riotous blooms that now graced the once barren flower beds.

"Would you look at that, Mom? Mrs. Calloway is coming back next month. She left such a lovely review." Amelia's voice was tinged with pride as she pointed to the booking.

"Her words were kinder than I ever expected," Charlotte whispered, fingertips tracing the screen. Inside her chest, a small knot of anxiety loosened, the unease that clung to her like morning fog dissipating just a bit more. It was more than the fresh coat of paint or the new furniture that signaled progress; it was the seeing how others appreciated this place the way Charlotte did.

They stashed their day's treasures and moved through to the common area, where Amelia set a fire that crackled invitingly in the hearth. "Tomorrow, let's put some of the shells in a jar for the mantlepiece," she suggested.

"Perfect," Charlotte agreed. "It'll be like having a piece of the sea with us, even indoors."

As they sat in wingback chairs and enjoyed the fire, some tea, and generous plates of the Wellington leftover from the previous night, Charlotte's mind wandered to the future – not the distant, uncertain horizon, but the tangible tomorrow filled with the promise of continued growth and healing. The Crown stood firm around them, its old bones sighing and creaking as the day cooled. The house had been her leap of faith, her canvas to transform, and now it was becoming home, proof that she could start anew.

"Hey, Mom?" Amelia's voice pulled her from her reverie. "I'm really glad we did this today. Just you and me."

"Me too, darling. Come here," she murmured, opening her arms.

Amelia sank into the embrace, her presence a balm to Charlotte's soul. In the quiet of the living room, with the remnants of the day fading into twilight, they held each other close. There was no need for words; their bond spoke volumes.

"Love you, Mom," Amelia whispered against her shoulder.

"Love you more, my girl," Charlotte replied, her voice steady even as emotion thickened her throat. Then, grinning against Amelia's hair, she added in her most serious voice, "Now, do you want to paint or do plumbing tomorrow?

Amelia's laughter was only slightly muffled against Charlotte's shoulder.

CHAPTER THREE

The afternoon sun cast a golden hue across the newly polished floors of The Crown Inn, transforming the lobby into a tapestry of light and shadow. Laughter bubbled from the lounge where Charlotte's newest guests congregated around the hearth, its crackling fire offering comfort. It was an ordinary yet bustling day at the inn, with each ring of the brass bell above the door heralding new arrivals seeking refuge in this coastal haven. So far, Charlotte had two of her four available rooms filled, and the couple currently admiring the fireplace was her third and final check-in for the week.

"Darling, look at this place! It's *charming,* isn't it?" Mrs. Harrison's voice cut through the congenial silence like a knife through butter. Charlotte, stationed behind the reception desk, smiled in greeting as the American couple approached from the formal living room.

"Quite," Mr. Harrison agreed, though his eyes darted about as if cataloging every detail for future scrutiny. His gaze sharpened and swung to Charlotte. "We expect our stay to be nothing short of exemplary."

"Of course, Mr. and Mrs. Harrison," Charlotte replied, her tone warm but tinged with wariness. She had a *feeling* about this couple. "We will do everything we can to ensure your comfort."

Mrs. Harrison propped designer sunglasses atop her head, revealing eyes that were keen and assessing. "We've traveled quite extensively," she announced, as if bestowing a challenge. "And we know what we like."

"Absolutely." Charlotte nodded. She stood behind the polished oak reception desk, a beacon of calm in the eye of the check-in storm. The Crown Inn hummed with activity, its walls echoing with laughter and chatter, yet she remained focused on the couple before her. The Harrisons had an air about them, one that spoke of accustomed luxury and unspoken—but exacting—expectations.

She regretted letting Amelia sleep in—Amelia would have loved to gawk at the Harrisons and their pretentious flashiness. They had come from Los Angeles, the same as the poetry book, but the Harrisons were decidedly less of a welcome find. Charlotte had plunged into innkeeping to stitch together a life frayed by divorce, and every satisfied guest was a patch in her quilt of reinvention—but the Harrisons, with their air of entitlement, threatened to tug at her stitching.

"Your room is ready," Charlotte assured them, hoping her efforts at online marketing hadn't attracted guests whose expectations towered above the quaint charm of The Crown Inn.

"Let's hope so," Mr. Harrison said, leaning in, a whiff of expensive cologne enveloping Charlotte. "We're here to relax, not to wait."

"Indeed," Charlotte echoed, her smile unyielding as she handed them their key. Inside, she felt the stirrings of a familiar resolve, the kind that had propelled her across the ocean to start anew. She had a feeling that Mr. Harrison was waiting for her to react to his sharpness, but he underestimated her. Their presence was a test—one she intended to pass with grace.

"Would it be too much trouble to have some extra towels sent up to our room?" Mrs. Harrison asked, twirling a strand of hair around her finger. Her voice was honeyed but carried an edge of command.

"Of course not, Mrs. Harrison," Charlotte responded with practiced ease, her fingers already dancing across the computer keyboard to note the request. "We want you to feel as comfortable as possible."

Mr. Harrison interjected, his tone less dulcet, more direct. "And the room must be kept at exactly seventy-two degrees. We find that to be the optimal sleeping temperature."

"Absolutely," Charlotte replied, her internal monologue recounting the steps she would take to achieve this precise climate control. She imagined herself like the artist she was, carefully mixing colors—only now she blended amenities and accommodations to create the perfect guest experience.

"Lastly, we adhere to a very strict diet—gluten-free, dairy-free, and we prefer organic fruits." Mrs. Harrison's eyes locked onto Charlotte's, searching for any hint of hesitation.

"Your dietary needs will be given our utmost attention," Charlotte assured them, her thoughts tumbling like waves against Chesham Cove's rocky shore. She considered the local suppliers, the freshest produce, visualizing the breakfast spread that would satisfy these stringent requirements.

"Very well," Mrs. Harrison said with a curt nod, the ghost of a smile gracing her lips. "We appreciate your... flexibility."

"Flexibility" was a word Charlotte had come to embrace in her new life. But she had a feeling that the Harrisons were about as flexible as an iron fence. As they departed toward the grand staircase, she made a mental checklist of everything needed to cater to their demands.

Charlotte lingered at the reception desk, her fingers tracing the grooves of the polished oak as she listened to the Harrisons ascend the stairs, their conversation a murmur lost in the grandeur of the foyer. The Crown Inn buzzed with the gentle hum of other guests settling in, yet Charlotte's attention remained fixed on the distant echo of the American couple's footsteps. A frown creased her forehead as she contemplated the precarious balance between accommodation and capitulation. She envisioned the scathing review that might spread like wildfire across the internet, tarnishing the reputation she'd so painstakingly built.

With a deep breath that did little to quell the tide of apprehension, Charlotte turned from the desk and made her way to the sanctuary of her office—a small room tucked away behind the scenes, filled with the comforting scent of lavender and aged paper. She sank into the embrace of her high-backed chair, the leather cool against her skin, and booted up the computer, its screen casting a soft glow in the dimly lit space.

Her inbox greeted her with the fruits of her labors: a string of new reservations scattered over the summer months and her first glowing testimonials from travelers who'd already stayed within the Crown Inn's walls. She clicked through to the message, the five-star rating and heartfelt comment warming her from within.

"Look at this, Amelia," she whispered, though her daughter was not there to hear. "They love what we've done with the place."

Her gaze swept over the numbers, imagining the steady climb of occupancy rates, and the future peaks of seasonal bookings. It was all there in black and white—the validation of her vision, the affirmation that her impulsive leap across the Atlantic had been more than just a flight of fancy.

Daniel would have said something derisive—just as he always had with her painting. But there was no criticism ringing in her ears now. Even amid the digital praise, though, the specter of the Harrisons' potential dissatisfaction loomed large. Charlotte reread the new review, which praised the inn's 'exceptional personal service,' and her throat tightened.

We cannot afford to slip, she thought, her fingers drumming a staccato rhythm on the desk. "Not now. Not with so much at stake."

She stood, paced before the window that framed a view of the untamed garden, its wildflowers swaying in the coastal wind. The Crown Inn was a living thing, and she, its caretaker, had coaxed it back to health. Yet, like any creature, it needed constant nurturing to thrive.

Turning from the window, Charlotte gathered the notes she had scribbled about the Harrisons' needs. Almond milk and no-gluten bread. She would need to visit town.

"Mom?" Amelia's voice pulled Charlotte from her reverie. She turned to find her daughter in the doorway, dressed but not quite looking awake.

A smile danced on Charlotte's lips. "Ah, she lives?" she mused. "Sleep well?"

Amelia closed the distance between them. "Yes," she conceded, "like a log. Way better than at the dorms. It's bustling out in the main house! You should have heard the couple in room six gushing about the four-poster bed and the view of the garden."

"High praise indeed," Charlotte acknowledged, her gaze drifting to the doorway. There were so many other rooms with spectacular views, just waiting to be renovated and put to use. But time—and money—were limiting factors. "We should start on the east wing next, don't you think?"

"Come on, let's take a walk outside," Amelia suggested, nudging Charlotte toward the French doors that led to the gardens. "Fresh air, and you can tell me about your plans for the east wing."

Together, they stepped out into the sunlight, the breeze tousling their hair as they walked along the manicured pathways interspersed with wildflowers. Charlotte's gaze lingered on the building that represented her new beginning.

"Look at it, Amelia," she murmured, pride threading through her words. "It's already so much more than I imagined when I first laid eyes on it."

Amelia squeezed her mother's hand. "It's not just the inn that's transformed, Mom. You are too."

Charlotte allowed herself a moment to bask in the truth of Amelia's observation before the practicalities of running an establishment reasserted themselves. The Harrisons, those demanding guests, would be expecting everything to be perfect. She could almost hear Mr. Harrison's brusque tone, requesting his myriad specifics for comfort. Charlotte quickly caught Amelia up on the morning's drama.

Amelia's eyebrows rose. "Wow, high maintenance much?"

"You have no idea," Charlotte replied with a wry smile. "But we'll manage. They're just... particular," she said, choosing her words carefully. "So I need to head to town to get a few things. You want to come?"

Amelia shook her head. "I was going to gather shells. Maybe head into town later. But you go on."

Something prickled at the back of Charlotte's mind at the casualness of Amelia's tone, but she brushed it aside. Charlotte nodded, understanding her daughter's desire for a bit of solitude. "Alright. Make sure to have some breakfast before you go, okay? There's fresh fruit and yogurt in the kitchen."

Amelia smiled, a hint of mischief in her eyes. "I will. And I'll leave some for the Harrisons."

Charlotte chuckled, appreciating her daughter's lighthearted approach to the situation. "Thank you. I've got to grab a few things from the kitchen, but then I'll be back soon."

With a final squeeze of Amelia's hand, Charlotte hustled back into the house. In the kitchen, she took a picnic basket from the cupboard. Today, she was packing a classic Cornish pasty, its flaky crust cradling a hearty blend of beef, potatoes, and swede. Her heart fluttered like the wings of a caged bird at the thought of Simon tasting her creations. Her mind wandered to Simon's rugged hands—so adept at mending nets and guiding his boats through churning waves—perhaps cradling her pasty with an approving nod. A smile tugged at the corners of her lips. He was kind, handsome, and so very English, a far cry from Daniel with his New York polish and predictable routines.

With the pasties wrapped up, Charlotte turned her attention to the coronation chicken, filling a lidded container with the creamy curry-infused sauce and tender chunks of poached chicken. She retrieved a crusty loaf of bread and some produce. She imagined Simon's surprise at the exotic yet homey taste. Charlotte arranged the lunch items with precision in the wicker basket lined with a red-and-white checkered cloth. She nestled the pasties next to a mason jar of pickled onions and a wedge of mature Cheddar cheese, the sharpness of which would complement the rich meaty pies. She placed the coronation chicken and other ingredients for sandwiches in, making sure not to forget the crisp lettuce leaves in parchment paper.

Will he appreciate this? she pondered, her hands hesitating as they arranged a small pot of clotted cream next to a cluster of fresh strawberries. It was all so different from anything Daniel would have eaten, but Simon wasn't Daniel. He appreciated the rugged cliffs and wild seas of Chesham Cove; perhaps he'd appreciate this too.

"Can't forget these," Charlotte added, slipping a pair of Bakewell tarts into the basket. Their sweet almond frangipane and raspberry jam filling would be the perfect end to their meal.

She stepped back, taking in the sight of her carefully curated offering. Pride swelled within her chest—a pride mingled with a dash of trepidation. She secured the basket's lid and hoisted the basket, feeling the weight of hope resting comfortably in its woven depths.

As she turned to leave and headed toward her car, her mind already ran through the list of items she needed to pick up for the Harrisons. And as Charlotte drove away, her thoughts lingered on Amelia's sudden desire for solitude. It was unlike her to pass up a trip into town. Was there more to Amelia's request to be alone? Was she simply enjoying some quiet time, or was there something else on her mind?

Shaking off the concern for the moment, Charlotte focused on the task at hand. She knew she could talk to Amelia later, perhaps over dinner, and gently probe if anything was amiss. For now, the priority was ensuring the Harrisons' stay at The Crown Inn was as comfortable and complaint-free as possible.

CHAPTER FOUR

As Charlotte parked outside the grocer's in Chesham, her phone dinged with a message. She checked it absently as she climbed out of the car, and her breath caught when she saw an email from the ancestry website she had been frequenting as of late.

Could it be?

"Probably nothing," she murmured to herself. And when the message turned out to be a renewal reminder, she whispered, "Just be patient." The words were a mantra, a lifeline that she had grasped through the tumult of divorce and change. They were also a promise, one that extended beyond the inn's restoration to the mending of her own fragmented history—the message had not been one from her father, nor had it contained any hint of where he might be. The mystery lingered.

Charlotte's fingers hesitated above the glossy screen of her smartphone, a modern oracle that remained stubbornly silent. The device lay cold and unyielding in her palm, its surface reflecting the pale morning light filtering through the lace curtains. She swiped through her other notifications with a flicker of impatience—the usual promotional emails, a reminder for an online art supplies sale, but nothing of the substance she sought. No whispers or digital breadcrumbs leading to her father. Her thumb hovered over the refresh icon, willing it to reveal some clue, any clue, but the inbox remained as barren as before. No new news.

"Nothing," she murmured, the word dissolving into the quiet air, tinged with disappointment.

Perhaps Sally has heard something, she thought, envisioning the bakery's warm glow and the scent of fresh bread as an antidote to the uncertainty gnawing at her heart. A restless energy propelled her forward past the grocer's, the soles of her boots clicking against the sidewalk. Charlotte knew that Sally, with her flour-dusted apron and ever-percolating pot of community news, might hold the key to the longed-for family reunion.

With each step toward the high street, Charlotte wrapped herself tighter in the cocoon of hope that had begun to unfurl within her chest. It was a delicate thing, easily torn, yet it pushed her past storefronts and the greetings of locals with optimism in her heart.

With each step along the cobblestone streets, she admired the quaint cottages, their gardens a riot of colors, bursting with life—a stark contrast to the sterile high rises of New York.

"Morning, Charlotte!" called Mr. Jenkins from his perch outside the corner shop, his newspaper folded neatly under his arm.

"Good morning," she replied with a smile, her American accent still drawing the occasional curious glance, even after months in the cove.

"Beautiful day, isn't it?" he remarked, his eyes twinkling behind spectacles that had seen many a sunny morning in this little town.

"Absolutely stunning," she agreed, her gaze lingering on the azure expanse of the sky, a canvas she longed to capture in oil and pigment.

Ambling past the flower shop, she waved to Mrs. Donnelly, who was arranging a bouquet of dahlias, their vibrant hues spilling out onto the pavement like drops of paint from an artist's palette. "Lovely blooms!" Charlotte called out.

"Thanks, love! Just wait 'til you see the roses," Mrs. Donnelly beamed, her pride in her work unmistakable.

Charlotte's heart swelled at these small exchanges; they were the threads that tethered her to this place. But beneath the surface of pleasantries, her mind churned with thoughts of the father she barely knew—a mystery man whose recent alleged sighting in London, according to her Cousin Agnes here in Chesham, had sparked a fire of curiosity within her.

"Morning, Charlotte!" called Mr. Henley from his perch outside the post office, his voice cutting through the solitude of her thoughts.

"Good morning, Mr. Henley!" she replied, her voice laced with polite warmth.

"Off to see Sally?" he ventured, his knowing eyes twinkling behind thick spectacles.

"Indeed, I am. Hoping she's got some fresh scones left," Charlotte answered with a small smile, though her stomach churned not with hunger, but with anticipation.

"Best hurry then. You know how quickly they disappear," he chuckled, returning to his newspaper.

"Will do. Have a good day," Charlotte tossed over her shoulder, hastening her pace.

The door to the bakery chimed cheerfully as she entered. The space was alive with the rhythmic dance of Sally's practiced movements—tending to the oven, sliding a tray of golden croissants onto the counter, brushing a lock of hair from her forehead with the back of her hand.

"Ah, there she is, our own New Yorker!" Sally exclaimed, placing the tray down with a clatter. "What can I get for you today, dear?"

"Just your delightful company, Sally," Charlotte quipped, though her eyes betrayed the true purpose of her visit. She leaned against the counter, observing the ebb and flow of patrons—each familiar face a reminder that she was no longer an outsider, but part of this community.

"Busy as ever, I see," she noted, her voice tinged with the lightest strain of fatigue—not from the early hour, but from the weight of unanswered questions that lingered at the back of her mind.

"Always, love. Can't have the good folks of Chesham Cove starting their day without a proper bit of sustenance," Sally responded, casting a knowing glance at Charlotte. "But you're not here for my scones, are you? You've got that look about you—the same one when you decided to buy that old inn."

Sally's observation drew a soft chuckle from Charlotte, the sound dancing amidst the clinking ceramics and hushed conversations. "You know me too well," she admitted, her fingers tracing the grain of the wooden countertop. "I'm searching for pieces of a puzzle that's been missing far too many bits."

Charlotte's words hung in the air, suspended like the fine dust motes caught in the sunbeams streaming through the front window.

"Ah, let me guess. Looking for a bit of gossip to go with your coffee?" Sally teased, placing a scone on a plate and pushing it across the counter with a wink.

"Something like that," Charlotte conceded, accepting the scone. "Actually, I was hoping you might've heard anything about my father?"

Sally's brows knitted together in concentration, her lips pursed as she sifted through the myriad of conversations stored in her mental archives. The pause stretched between them, filled with the clinking of cups and the murmur of patrons enjoying their morning reprieve.

"Henry? Sorry, love. Haven't heard hide nor hair about him," Sally finally said, her tone apologetic. "But you'll be the first to know if I do. Nothing from your cousin Agnes, then?"

"No, unfortunately not. And she's usually the one he bunks with when he blows into town. Thank you, Sally. I appreciate it," Charlotte replied.

In the quiet aftermath of thwarted hopes, Charlotte bit into the buttery scone, its flakiness a small comfort. She looked around the bakery, taking solace in the steady rhythm of life that pulsed around her—a life she had chosen, and one that was supposed to have quieted all of her turmoil. But there was still the lingering question of her estranged father's whereabouts—and the years-old questions of why Henry Anderson had become a ghost, separate from his family, his silence as telling as though he had actually died.

Tomorrow is another day, she reminded herself. *And I'll keep searching, one scone, one rumor at a time.*

"Charlotte," Sally finally said after a beat. The other woman's eyes held hers for a heartbeat, two. "Let's sit down for a minute, dear." Sally gestured toward a small table tucked away in the corner, away from the lingering customers. The simple act of sitting seemed to bear the weight of ceremony, and Charlotte followed, her movements mirroring Sally's own—smooth and deliberate.

As they settled, the symphony of the bakery resumed around them—the quiet rustle of paper bags, the gentle clink of China, the muted conversations of patrons lost in their own worlds. Charlotte's gaze remained fixed on Sally, her heart thrumming a silent drum of hope against the stillness of her exterior.

"Rumors come and go like the tide here," Sally began. "But if there's anything to be known, Charlotte, trust that you'll be the first I tell."

Charlotte nodded, her lips curving into a half-smile that didn't quite reach her eyes. She clasped her hands together, feeling the cool press of her wedding band—a token of a life she had left behind. She wasn't quite sure why she hadn't taken it off. She realized, in a moment of shock, that she now had no use for the ring.

"Ah, well," Charlotte murmured, her gaze drifting to the window where morning light danced upon the glass in playful patterns. "Maybe it's for the best." She watched as a couple strolled by, their laughter seeping through the bakery walls, threading through the air with an easiness that tugged at something wistful within her.

"Anything else stirring in Chesham Cove?" Charlotte asked, her voice lilting into a more casual tone, inviting the kind of chatter that filled the spaces between searching and finding.

"Stirring? Always," Sally chuckled, leaning back into her chair, the familiar creak sounding like an old tune played on a well-loved fiddle. "Let's see, the Brown twins have started walking now. Little terrors, they are—into everything."

"Twins have a special sort of magic," Charlotte mused, a smile finally lighting up her face as she pictured the toddlers' shared mischief. "Double the trouble, but twice the joy, I'd imagine."

"Indeed," Sally agreed, eyes twinkling. "And did you hear about Mr. Fletcher's prize roses? The blue ribbons this year went straight to his head, he's been parading around like a peacock!"

Their laughter mingled, and Charlotte found solace; the ebb and flow of village life provided an anchor amidst her own tumultuous sea of emotions.

"Peacocks and roses," Charlotte echoed thoughtfully, a wry grin appearing. "The tamest of drama. Things never change around here, do they?"

"Speaking of changes," Sally continued, lowering her voice conspiratorially, "have you seen the renovations they're doing over at the vicarage? Quite modern. It's got some of the old guard in a tizzy!"

"Change can be good," Charlotte replied softly, her gaze turning inward. "Sometimes it's the only way to find what we're looking for." Her fingers traced the rim of her teacup, circling round and round—a physical manifestation of her thoughts spiraling toward possibilities yet unseen.

"True enough," Sally nodded, her wise eyes locking onto Charlotte's. "Except Thomas Windnell's place. Not a one here in Chesham happy about that place. A monster of a hotel, it is. And getting bigger! I swear, every time you put on a new shingle at The Crown, Windnell adds another wing to his behemoth."

Charlotte's smile faltered at the mention of Thomas Windnell's sprawling resort. The image of the grand, ever-expanding hotel down the coast from Chesham loomed in her mind, casting a shadow over her quaint, beloved Crown Inn. The man himself—who she'd had a few unfortunate run-ins with—seemed a brilliant businessman but a rotten person. He seemed to only see dollar signs and not the people he would be affecting in Chesham with his megahotel. They had developed a mutual distaste for one another. She set her teacup down with a gentle clink, her fingers lingering on the porcelain, suddenly cold.

"Windnell's resort," she echoed, her voice carrying a hint of unease. The thought of that corporate giant, with its endless resources and appeal to a different class of clientele, gnawed at her. Charlotte had poured her heart into The Crown Inn, nurturing it into a haven. But could it withstand the competition from Windnell's impersonal yet luxurious titan?

Her mind raced with troubled thoughts. The Crown Inn was more than just a business; it was a symbol of her new life, her resilience, her passion. It represented everything she had worked so hard to build and become. The idea of Windnell's resort overshadowing her efforts, luring away potential guests with its flashy allure, was disheartening.

Charlotte forced a smile, trying to mask the sudden surge of worry. "Well, The Crown has its own charm, doesn't it? We cater to those who seek a more personal touch, a bit of history and heart."

Sally nodded, her expression understanding. "That's true, love. The Crown has something special that no fancy hotel can replicate. But Windnell's place... it's changing the landscape around here. Not just physically, but... the feel of the village."

Charlotte sighed, her heart heavy. The challenge was greater than she had anticipated. It wasn't just about maintaining her business; it was about preserving the essence of Chesham Cove, the very thing that had drawn her to this place. She would need to be clever, resourceful, and perhaps even a little bold to ensure The Crown Inn not only survived but thrived in the shadow of Windnell's place.

"Well, we just won't let that happen, will we, Sally?" Charlotte offered a small smile, her mind racing. She rose from the stool. Her movements were deliberate. "Thank you for the chat and the company. And the scone."

"Anytime, love," Sally replied, her warm smile a beacon in the cozy bakery.

As she stepped out of the bakery, the cool breeze kissed Charlotte's cheeks, whispering promises of revelations to come. With each footfall on the cobblestone street, Charlotte reaffirmed to herself that this search for her father was not in vain, that every small interaction, every piece of gossip, might be a breadcrumb leading her—and maybe him—home.

The cobblestones gave way to a cushion of golden sand as Charlotte Moore stepped onto the beach, the morning light casting her shadow long and slender beside her. She wrapped her cardigan tighter against her body, not out of cold but comfort, as the salt-laden breeze played with wisps of her auburn hair. The rhythmic cadence of crashing waves provided an ambient soundtrack to her thoughts. With each step, the sand yielded gently beneath her boots, a soft surrender to her measured pace.

"Beautiful, isn't it?" she mused aloud to no one in particular, her voice barely rising above the whisper of the sea. "How endless it all seems."

She stopped, allowing the serenity to envelop her, watching as gulls swooped low, their cries punctuating the steady hush of water. It was here, amid the vastness of ocean and sky, that Charlotte felt the weight of her quest lighten. Her father's presence seemed both near and far, like the horizon itself—intangible yet ever-present.

"Maybe you're out there," she whispered, eyes tracing the line where blue met blue. "Watching the same sun rise."

With a sigh lodged in her throat, Charlotte turned and resumed her walk, this time back to the grocer's for the Harrisons' culinary supplies. An idea came to her as she walked, one that brightened up her tumultuous emotions. She was reminded of the basket she had packed back at The Crown. She would push aside her worries and, after the grocer's, she would go to see Simon at the harbor.

CHAPTER FIVE

Amidst the bustling scene at Chesham's harbor, Simon stood out like a lighthouse. He moved across the deck of his boat with an easy grace, his hands sure and steady as they coiled a rope with practiced efficiency. His weathered skin told tales of countless hours under the sun and wind, and his eyes held the depth of the ocean, reflecting both its calm and its storms.

Chesham Cove's port area was a circus of motion and sound, a living portrait of seaside life where the salty tang of the sea intermingled with the cries of seagulls. The fishing boats, painted in hues of blues and reds, bobbed gently on the water's surface, their masts swaying like dancers to the rhythm of the lapping waves. Nets lay stretched out on the docks, shimmering with droplets from their latest voyage, while lobster pots stacked in towers promised future bounties.

"Oi, Simon! That new net holding up alright?" called a fellow fisherman from a neighboring vessel.

"Like a dream," Simon replied, his voice carrying over the water, a rich baritone that seemed to resonate with the very timbers of his boat. "Best one in the fleet now, thanks to your handiwork."

He gave the net a final tug and turned his attention to a wooden crate filled with freshly caught fish, their scales glinting like silver coins. With an ease that spoke of years in the trade, he began sorting through the catch, setting aside the finest specimens with a discerning eye.

"Good haul today, then?" came another voice, this one tinged with the lilt of local gossip.

"Decent enough," Simon responded without looking up, his focus never wavering from his task. "The sea's been generous."

Charlotte's pulse quickened, the weight of the picnic basket in her hand a comforting anchor against her fluttering heart. The scent of salt and sea intertwining with the lingering aroma of her meticulously prepared lunch created an intoxicating mixture that seemed to charge the air around her. With every step closer to the water's edge, her anticipation grew, tinged with a nervousness that made her hands tremble slightly beneath the cloth napkin protecting her culinary creations. What if he didn't like the food?

"Simon!" she called out, her voice barely rising above the coastal din as she approached the moored boats. He turned at the sound of his name, his expression shifting from concentration to curiosity when he spotted Charlotte making her way toward him.

"Charlotte! What brings you down to the docks? Not fleeing the country, I hope? Too homesick for America? Decided the weather's too unpredictable in England?" His voice boomed with good-natured humor, the corners of his mouth lifting into a grin that softened the lines of his weather-beaten face.

"Very funny," she retorted, the playfulness in her tone belying the butterflies performing acrobatics in her stomach. "Actually, I've brought something for you." She presented the basket with a flourish, watching as Simon's brow rose in skeptical surprise.

"Is that so?" He eyed the wicker container warily as if it might contain a live eel rather than lunch. "What do we have here then? More of your... 'experimental' British cuisine?"

"Experimental?" Charlotte feigned offense, though the twinkle in her eye betrayed her amusement. "I'll have you know these are classic recipes, lovingly crafted with my own two hands." She lifted the lid, revealing an array of dishes nestled among checked linens.

"I see cheese and... what is this, exactly?" Simon poked gingerly at a Cornish pasty, his expression dubious.

"Careful now, that pasty might just bite back," Charlotte teased, watching as Simon cautiously sniffed the pastry. "It's simple fare but hearty. Perfect for a hardworking man like yourself."

"Never had one before," he admitted, still peering at the meal with the caution of a man who'd spent his life trusting the familiar fruits of the sea over those of the land.

"Then today's your lucky day, Simon Harris. Prepare to be amazed." Her words were light, but inwardly she hoped her efforts would be well-received. She wasn't just offering food; she was sharing a part of herself, a gesture of care wrapped in pastry. And, owing to her past experience—and perhaps a little unfair to Simon—she braced herself for criticism.

"Right, let's give it a go then," Simon said, hopping to the pier and settling onto a nearby bench. She patted the space beside him. Charlotte joined him, the warmth of his presence doing little to calm the excited pounding of her heart.

As they sat side by side overlooking the serene blue waters of the harbor, Charlotte watched as Simon gingerly unfolded the crimped edge of the pasty, his blue eyes reflecting a mix of amusement and trepidation. She bit her lip to stifle a giggle, leaning forward slightly.

"Think of it as treasure wrapped in golden dough," she coaxed, her voice a playful lilt that danced on the salty breeze. "Only instead of gold doubloons, you get steak and potatoes."

"Treasure hunt on a bench by the harbor, eh?" His chuckle was rich and warm, the sea breeze ruffling the hair at the nape of his neck as he glanced at her with a spark of mirth in his gaze. "You do know how to tempt an old sea dog."

"Old? Please, you're in your prime, Captain Harris." Charlotte's retort was swift, matched only by the twinkle in her eye. "Besides, I'm quite certain this particular voyage won't lead to scurvy."

"Ah, well, if there's no risk of scurvy..." Simon finally took a cautious bite, his teeth sinking into the flaky crust with a satisfying crunch. The action held a hint of surrender, a silent admission that he was willing to cast off into unknown culinary waters for her sake. Daniel, especially in the latter years of their marriage, had simply stopped making any effort for her.

Charlotte watched intently as Simon chewed thoughtfully, and she could see his initial skepticism melting away as the rich gravy coated his palate, the meat succulent and the vegetables cooked to a comforting tenderness. The seasoning—just a touch of rosemary and thyme—complemented the savory filling.

"Blimey, that is good," he said after a moment, surprise etching his rugged features. His eyebrows, previously knit with doubt, now arched in genuine appreciation. "I stand corrected, Charlotte. This might just be better than my mum's Sunday roast."

"High praise coming from a man who's tasted the bounty of the sea his whole life." Her heart swelled at his words, warmth flooding her cheeks. To have her food likened to the sacred institution of a British Sunday meal was an unexpected victory.

"Your hands work magic, not just with paints but with pastries too," Simon continued, giving her cheek a kiss before taking another hearty bite. The corners of his mouth lifted in a contented smile, one that reached all the way to his eyes.

"Who knew?" He gestured with the half-eaten pasty, his gesture encompassing both the basket of food and, Charlotte felt, the budding connection between them.

She laughed, a sound that mingled with the cries of the gulls and the gentle lap of water against the hulls of the boats. "Well, I did hope you'd enjoy it. Consider it my bid to anchor myself here in Chesham Cove, through stomachs if nothing else."

"Anchor away, then," he replied, his voice rich with the promise of shared meals—and perhaps shared tomorrows. He looked at her warmly, a flicker of desire in the depths of his gaze. Charlotte felt herself blush.

As Simon continued to savor the lunch she'd prepared, the gentle hum of the harbor seemed to slow to a languorous tempo. Charlotte watched Simon lean back against the weathered wood of the bench, his eyes momentarily closed in appreciation. The sun, high and benevolent, cast a golden sheen on the scene, turning the simple lunch into a tableau of quiet contentment.

"Simon," Charlotte began, her tone light yet threaded with an undercurrent of excitement. "Have you ever thought about tours? On your boats, I mean." She twisted a strand of hair around her finger, a habit when she was mulling over artistic possibilities—or, as it seemed now, business ones. The idea of tours had been one they had spoken about before, and it seemed it might benefit them both.

His eyes widened, a hint of seafoam green meeting her earnest gaze. "Tours?" he echoed, the word hanging between them like a sail waiting for wind.

"Yes, like... like fishing expeditions for tourists. Or even just coastal cruises. People are always looking for experiences these days, aren't they? It could be a way to diversify, attract more customers."

A forkful of the Cornish pasty paused midway to Simon's mouth, and he set it down, a furrow appearing on his brow. His hands, still faintly scented with the ocean's brine, found their way to his chin, stroking the rough stubble there. Charlotte noted the hesitation that flickered across his features, the way his gaze drifted out toward the horizon, perhaps envisioning the risks as clearly as the endless blue before them.

"More customers, hm?" He considered her words, weighing them against the rhythm of his life that was as predictable and reassuring as the tides. "I have the occasional charter, but nothing steady. It's not a bad idea, Charlotte, but it's... well, it's different from hauling nets and setting lines."

"Sometimes different can be good," she offered, her voice a soft encouragement. "Think of all the untapped potential—"

"Potential that comes with complications," Simon interjected gently. His practical nature, the one that had ensured his boats weathered many a storm, now anchored him in caution. "Regulations, safety measures, insurance, not to mention the unpredictability of tourists."

"True," Charlotte conceded, her enthusiasm undiminished by his doubts. "But isn't that what life here has taught us? To embrace the unpredictable?"

He smiled then, a smile that mingled admiration with affection. "You do have a point, Charlotte. And I suppose I'd be lying if I said the idea doesn't hold a certain appeal."

"Imagine it," she pressed on, her hands gesturing as if painting the picture in the air before them. "The Old Crown Inn could even partner with you. We could offer packages—a room with a view and a day out at sea. It's collaboration, community."

Simon let out a soft chuckle, the sound blending with the cawing of the gulls overhead. He picked up the pasty once more, his appetite returning as he mulled over her proposal. "Collaboration and community, eh? Those are strong currents to sail on."

"Exactly!" Charlotte's heart swelled with hope, sensing the shift in his demeanor. "And think of the stories people will take back with them. Your Chesham Cove, shared with the world."

"Shared with the world..." he murmured, lost for a moment in the vision she had conjured. The man who knew every secret of the sea was now navigating uncharted waters, considering a voyage beyond his familiar shores.

"When people come here seeking the story they've heard, seeking the adventure, they bring their friends, their families. They eat at our inn, they sleep in our beds, they buy from our shops. Your sea becomes a siren's call, not just for fish, but for prosperity." She gestured into the air as if painting a picture.

Imon sat upright as if the potential of her vision had physically drawn him to his full height. He extended his hand, roughened from years at sea, an offering of partnership, of new horizons. "I'll consider it—properly. You make a compelling case, and truth be told, I'd like to see this place thrive too."

His words were more than mere acquiescence; they were the tender shoots of faith in her, in the shared venture that lay ahead. And as their hands met, the warmth of his palm pressed against hers, there was a silent acknowledgment of the mutual trust being threaded through their fingers.

"Thank you, Simon," Charlotte breathed out, her relief mixing with the tang of salt air. She felt the fluttering in her chest settle, replaced by a burgeoning sense of partnership, of unity. And something warmer and more intimate—definitely not business-related.

"But not right away. Let's just chew on it for a while," he finally said, a twinkle in his eye revealing that he was onboard with the idea, even if he hadn't quite hoisted the sails yet.

"Chewing is something we're both good at," Charlotte quipped, relief flooding through her as she reached for a tart, offering it to him with a playful flourish. "Especially today."

"Let's finish our lunch then, shall we?" he suggested with a chuckle, gesturing to the remnants of the food.

As they turned back to their meal, Charlotte watched as Simon's hands, still marked by the morning's work, deftly folded the wax paper around the remnants of her culinary experiment. His roughened fingers moved with unexpected grace—a contrast to the rugged intensity she had come to associate with his daily toil among the nets and boats.

"Simon," she began, her voice a soft effusion carried on the breeze, "I've been thinking about...well, about dreams. You know, the ones we're almost afraid to say out loud." She tucked a stray curl behind her ear, feeling suddenly vulnerable.

He paused, looking up from the neat parcel he had created. His eyes, the color of the ocean at twilight, held hers. "Go on," he encouraged gently.

She took a deep breath. "Back in New York, my dream was to create art that would touch people—change them somehow. And now that Daniel has set me free..." Her gaze drifted to The Old Crown Inn, perched like an ancient sentinel over Chesham Cove, the embodiment of her newfound aspirations.

"Freedom suits you," Simon said. He turned to face her, his hand reaching up to tuck a stray lock of hair behind her ear.

"Perhaps," Charlotte agreed, her heart swelling with the weight of possibilities, "but so does having an anchor." Her gaze traveled from the boats bobbing in the harbor to the man beside her—the one who had become her steadfast harbor in this quaint English seaside town.

"An anchor can be good—as long as it lets you sail when you need to," Simon replied, his tone carrying both the wisdom of a man of the sea and the tenderness of a man in love. "I don't ever want you to feel like I would hold you back from your dreams."

She watched a fisherman hauling in his catch, the silvery fish flashing in the sunlight before disappearing into the hold. There was a rhythm here, a cycle of ebb and flow that mirrored her own journey. From the chaos of her life in New York to the unexpected sanctuary she'd found in Chesham Cove, everything seemed to be aligning, much like the tides governed by the moon's pull.

"Before I came here, I never realized how much I needed... this," Charlotte said, her hand gesturing toward the serene harbor.

"Nature has a way of healin' us without us even knowin'," he responded, a rugged hand capturing hers, his grasp firm yet gentle.

Her fingers curled around his, a smile playing on her lips. She let her thoughts drift, imagining their future together. The Old Crown Inn, once crumbling, now held promise, much like her relationship with Simon.

"And now?" Simon prompted, his curiosity piqued. "What do you dream of now?"

"Now, I dream of restoring The Old Crown to its former glory. To make it a place where people can find peace, maybe even a bit of themselves." Charlotte's thoughts unfolded before him, delicate and earnest. "But it's more than just the inn. It's this place, Chesham Cove, and all its possibilities. It's..." She hesitated, a blush warming her cheeks. "It's sharing these dreams with someone who understands."

"Charlotte," Simon said, his voice low, resonant with the pull of something deeper, "I reckon my dreams have always been about keeping the boats afloat, providing for me crew. But you've got me thinking bigger, dreaming of more than just the next catch." He reached out, taking her hand in his, the intimacy of the gesture sending ripples through her heart.

"More?" she echoed, her own hand instinctively tightening around his.

"More," he confirmed with a nod. "Like making Chesham not just a stopover but a destination for tourists. Your ideas for the business—they're good, Charlotte. They're more than just expanding; they're evolving."

A seagull cried overhead, a sound that seemed to underscore the moment—the turning of pages in the chapters of their lives. Charlotte felt a surge of joy, buoyed by the undercurrent of hope that flowed between them. And she felt joyous, understood by Simon in a way she never had in the past.

"Oi, none of that now," he chided softly, brushing a thumb across her cheek, catching a rebellious tear. "We're in this together, aren't we? This old anchor and you, love."

"Yes," she whispered, "together."

They sat in companionable silence, finishing their lunch as the sun warmed their backs and the future stretched before them.

"Ready to head back?" Simon's voice pulled her from her reverie.

"Almost," she said, taking a deep breath of the briny air. "Let's just stay a moment longer."

Together, they watched the sun dip lower, painting the sky in shades of orange and pink. The harbor's beauty was timeless, unmarred by the comings and goings of its transient visitors. For Charlotte, it was more than just a backdrop; it had become a part of her story, a place where healing had begun and love had taken root. She wanted to tell Simon about her stressful morning with the Harrisons, the talk with Sally, the frustration she felt at her father's lingering absence. But she didn't want to ruin this moment.

"I can't imagine being anywhere else," she confessed, her voice barely above a whisper.

"Nor can I," Simon said, pulling her closer. "You've brought life back to this old harbor, Charlotte. To me."

"Come over again tonight," she coaxed, nestling into him. "Will you?"

35

"Of course. How could I resist being anywhere you are?"

She smiled, but internally, her mind was a whirlwind of worries and doubts. She thought about her father, whose absence had left a gaping hole in her life. His silence was a constant source of pain and speculation, an unresolved chapter that often left her feeling adrift.

As she gazed out over the harbor, her eyes inevitably drifted to the ever-expanding silhouette of Thomas Windnell's resort, a faint outline down the coast. Its imposing presence was an annoying reminder of the challenges facing her beloved Crown Inn. The thought of competing against such a colossal establishment brought fear.

Then there were her own aspirations for The Crown. Charlotte harbored dreams of restoring it to its former glory, as she'd said, of turning it into a haven for those in search of peace and a touch of home. But with Windnell's looming expansion, those dreams felt increasingly threatened. And with guests like The Harrisons, might she be doomed to cater to impossible patrons in increasing numbers? Doubts crept in about her ability to safeguard the future of her little sanctuary amidst such formidable factors.

Beside her, Simon sat in quiet support, his presence a comforting constant. She appreciated his companionship, his unspoken understanding. For a moment, Charlotte considered voicing her fears, seeking solace in shared concerns. But she held back, not wishing to disturb the tranquility of their shared moment with her inner turmoil.

CHAPTER SIX

The late afternoon sun bathed The Old Crown Inn in a golden hue, casting long shadows across the lush garden. In the formal living room, sorting through boxes she had brought down from the attic, Charlotte's fingers traced the spine of a leather-bound guestbook that had seen better days, much like the inn itself. She sighed, allowing herself a rare moment of reflection. It was then that the front door creaked open with defined self-importance, heralding the arrival of *Thomas Windnell.*

"Ah, The Crown," Thomas announced, his voice dripping with feigned delight as he stepped into the foyer, eyes quickly appraising. "Still standing, I see. How quaint."

Windnell wore a tailored navy blue suit that fit him impeccably, accentuating his stature. The suit was likely from a high-end designer, its fabric rich and smooth, suggesting a blend of fine wool and silk. He wore a crisp white shirt underneath, its collar perfectly starched, peeking just so above the lapel of his jacket. The shirt was fastened with what appeared to be custom-made cufflinks, subtle yet undeniably expensive, glinting in the sunlight streaming through the window.

Around his neck was a silk tie, patterned in a tasteful, understated design, knotted impeccably. It was complemented by a pocket square neatly folded in his suit's breast pocket, adding a splash of coordinated color that spoke of a man who paid attention to the finer details. Charlotte wondered if he was paying attention to the small detail of her spike of annoyance at his intrusion.

On his feet were polished leather shoes, shining so brightly they almost reflected the room. The shoes were of a classic style, well-maintained and suggesting both comfort and luxury. To complete his ensemble, Thomas wore a sleek, high-end watch on his wrist, its face simple yet elegant, the band made of fine leather or perhaps even a discreet metal, indicative of his preference for quality and understatement. Not that anyone would have seen him and not known that the man screamed money.

His overall appearance was one of cultivated sophistication, a man who understood the power of a well-tailored suit and the statement it made in both business and social circles. As he stood in the foyer of The Old Crown Inn, Charlotte was painfully aware of the disparity between his world and the one she had embraced.

Charlotte tightened her grip on the guestbook, her knuckles whitening. Forced a polite smile. "Thomas. What an unexpected...pleasure."

One corner of Thomas's mouth quirked upward. "Well, I must say, Charlotte, you've done wonders with the place." His gaze swept over her, the compliment laced with something less flattering. "Considering what you had to work with."

She watched as he strolled leisurely through the lobby, his shoes clicking against the stone floor. Each step seemed to echo not just in the space but within her, each tap a reminder of the battles she faced in preserving the house.

"Such a...rustic charm," Thomas continued, running a finger along the reception desk and inspecting the dust it gathered. "Very...you."

"Rustic is one word for it," Charlotte replied, maintaining her composure despite the rising irritation.

"Indeed," Thomas said, leaning closer to examine a crack in the wood paneling. "But I suppose it's all about potential, isn't it? Though I doubt many would see it beneath all this...character."

"Character is what we're known for here at The Crown," Charlotte countered, her tone measured. She followed him as he moved into the main parlor, where mismatched furniture sat awaiting reupholstery.

"Of course," he mused, picking up a cushion and grimacing at the outdated pattern before setting it down again. "It's just that, with the right investment, this could all be so much more modern. Profitable, even."

"Modern isn't always synonymous with better, Thomas. Some people appreciate the authenticity of a place like this." Her words were steeped in defiance, though inwardly, she felt the weight of his criticisms. "What is it that you came for?"

Thomas chuckled softly, almost affectionately, as if he found her naiveté endearing. And he ignored her question. "Authenticity is such a subjective term, don't you think?"

"Perhaps," she allowed, watching him as he peered out of the window at the view—the very coastline he planned to commercialize. "But there are some things money can't replace. Like integrity. Or respect for the land."

"Ah, but money does make the world go round, dear Charlotte. And progress is inevitable." He turned from the window, his sharp gaze locking onto hers. "Best to be on the right side of it."

With those parting words, Thomas Windnell sauntered back toward the entrance, pausing at the door. She wrapped her arms around herself, feeling the chill that had nothing to do with the drafty old room. The warmth of the sun outside now seemed worlds away.

"Charlotte, I must commend you," Thomas said, his voice smooth like polished silver, yet with an edge that could cut. "It takes a certain... bravery to cling to the past this way."

"Thank you, *Thomas,*" Charlotte replied, her words measured and cool despite the tempest brewing in her chest. "For your compliment and your brief, yet bizarre visit."

"Of course," he continued, leaning against the worn wooden doorframe with deceptive casualness, "one can't help but wonder if such bravery is really just a stubborn refusal to adapt." His smile was a razor, hidden beneath silk.

"Adaptation doesn't require surrender," she countered, meeting his eyes firmly, letting him see the steel beneath her veneer of poise.

He chuckled, shaking his head as he straightened his tailored jacket. "Well, I'll leave you to your... quaint endeavors. Just remember, there's a fine line between a dream and a delusion. When you're ready for reality, I'll be around."

As the door closed behind him, the sound echoed hollowly in the expanse of the inn's entrance hall. Charlotte let out a breath she hadn't realized she'd been holding, her fingers trembling. The tightness in her shoulders eased fractionally, but her heart still pounded an uneven rhythm. What had been his aim in coming here—to intimidate her?

She glanced at the door, half-expecting Thomas to reappear with another jab aimed to undermine her. But the entryway remained empty, the silence oppressive. She turned back to the reception desk, surveying the aging wood that gleamed under years of polish and care—a testament to resilience, much like herself.

"Mom?" Amelia's voice drifted from the staircase, a lifeline thrown in the quiet aftermath of Thomas Windnell's visit.

"In here, darling," Charlotte called, her voice steady despite the fresh doubts Thomas had planted in her mind. It was one thing to combat the decay of time, quite another to fight off the assault of a man like Windnell—handsome, refined, and devastatingly effective at sowing seeds of uncertainty.

She would not let him see her falter, not now, not ever. Yet as she resumed her tasks, the dissonance of his words lingered, an unwelcome guest all their own.

Amelia appeared, and her eyes widened when she saw Charlotte. "I heard someone down here. A man's voice. Did he upset you?" Amelia's question, innocent and perceptive, made Charlotte pause. She looked at her daughter, the future she fought for, and forced a smile.

"No, not at all," she lied gently, pressing a kiss to Amelia's forehead. "It was Thomas Windnell. Just his usual business talk."

"Okay," Amelia said slowly, doubt in her voice. "I was going to wade along the shore, maybe read at the beach. Want to come?"

"No, dear. Thanks for the invite. I have to prep some things in the kitchen for our *particular guests*."

Amelia giggled and scampered away, and Charlotte's gaze fell once again to the doorway where Thomas had exited, and the tiny fissure in her armor ached—a reminder of the fragility of new beginnings and the relentless tide of change threatening to sweep them away.

The last echoes of Thomas Windnell's caustic laughter had barely faded when the door to The Crown creaked open, announcing a new presence. Charlotte steeled herself to see Windnell again, but through the archway, shafts of afternoon light streamed in, catching on the strands of golden hair that framed the face of the woman who entered—a vision so startlingly beautiful it seemed as if Aphrodite herself had traded the ocean's foam for the quaintness of Chesham Cove.

"Good afternoon," she said, her voice smooth and measured, with an enigmatic lilt that held notes of places far beyond the English coast.

Charlotte, now lingering by the reception desk, was struck by the woman's statuesque poise. She stood tall, her posture impeccable, draped in a fitted trench coat that reeked of elegance and class.

Charlotte couldn't help but feel dwarfed by this stranger's grace, especially when her own spirit felt so depleted from Thomas's barbs.

"Welcome to The Old Crown Inn," Charlotte replied, mustering a professional warmth. "May I have your name?"

"Of course." The woman's lips curved into a smile that didn't quite reach her eyes. "Isla Wagner."

"Ms. Wagner," Charlotte echoed, tapping the name into the aged computer with a practiced rhythm. The name sparked nothing in her memory, offering no clues as to why the hairs on the back of her neck stood on end. The inn's ledger hadn't mentioned anything about a Wagner due to arrive, and yet here she was—unexpected, unannounced, and undeniably unsettling.

"Is there a husband or family joining you?" Charlotte inquired, part of the check-in dance she'd learned since taking up the mantle of innkeeper.

"No, just me," Isla stated simply, shifting her weight ever so slightly, the movement fluid and intentional. Her gaze swept across the room, absorbing the details of the worn furniture and the paintings that Charlotte had lovingly hung upon the walls.

"Ah, I see." Charlotte nodded, hands clasping and unclasping beneath the desk. She felt exposed under Isla's scrutiny, vulnerable in a way she hadn't expected. This woman carried with her an air of mystery, and Charlotte found herself both intrigued and intimidated.

"We do have a single room left. Is there a specific reason you've chosen us for your stay?" Charlotte ventured, unable to contain her curiosity, though she would never let it show on her face.

"Let's call it a personal retreat," Isla responded, her tone noncommittal as she glanced out the window toward the craggy coastline. "This place has a certain... allure."

There was a depth to Isla's words that hinted at layers yet to be uncovered, and Charlotte could not shake the feeling that there was much more behind that serene facade. What sort of past did one need to escape from that led them to the doorstep of The Crown? Charlotte herself had come after personal tragedy, so she imagined all sorts of things that might have led Isla here.

"The room is already ready," Charlotte said, handing over a brass key with an ornate fob. "Dinner will be served at seven in the dining

41

hall. Sea bass is the catch of the day—it's quite lovely. How lon.
you planning to stay with us?"

"Thank you," Isla replied, accepting the key, her fingertips brushing
against Charlotte's hand—an unintentional touch that sent an
inexplicable shiver down Charlotte's spine. "I look forward to dinner."
She seemed to purposefully avoid answering the question of duration.

As Isla ascended the staircase, her silhouette cast long shadows
against the floral wallpaper, each step measured and sure. Charlotte
watched her disappear around the corner, a sense of unease coiling in
the pit of her stomach.

Who was Isla Wagner? And what had truly brought her to The
Crown? Charlotte shook her head gently, trying to dispel the disquiet
that clung to her like the mist rolling in from the sea. But try as she
might, Charlotte knew that some questions would demand answers,
whether she was prepared to hear them or not.

An hour later, the attic boxes were sorted and the late afternoon
light filtered through the bay windows of The Crown, casting a warm
glow that seemed to dance across the mahogany floorboards. Charlotte
busied herself straightening a stack of brochures on Chesham Cove's
local attractions and was updating the online bookings when Isla
reappeared, descending the staircase with the quiet grace of a wraith.

"Ms. Moore," she began, her voice smooth like clotted cream, "I
was wondering if you could tell me a bit about the history of this inn?"

Charlotte turned to face her guest, clasping her hands in front of her
to still their sudden tremble. The question, innocent as it was, felt
probing beneath Isla's intense gaze. "Certainly," she managed with a
practiced smile. "The Crown dates back to the 18th century. It served as
a private residence for a wealthy sea captain and his family—some say
he made his real money privateering—before being converted into an
inn almost a hundred years ago."

"Ah, I see," Isla said, tilting her head slightly as if studying an
intricate painting. "And what about you, Ms. Moore? Your accent hints
at a story far from English shores."

"New York originally," Charlotte replied, the words slipping out
with a hint of nostalgia. "But I suppose I was seeking a different kind
of life—slower, more deliberate." She paused, feeling the weight of
Isla's scrutiny. "Chesham Cove seemed like the perfect place to start
over."

"Starting over," Isla echoed softly, moving closer to examine a vase of fresh-cut peonies on the reception desk. "That's a brave choice."

Charlotte noted the way Isla's fingers traced the delicate petals, leaving them trembling gently in her wake. "Sometimes life doesn't give us much choice," she said, her voice dropping to a near whisper.

"Indeed," Isla murmured, her eyes lifting to meet Charlotte's own.

"Was there something particular you were escaping from?" The question, wrapped in the guise of casual conversation, struck a nerve. A chill ran down Charlotte's spine, mirroring the one from Isla's touch earlier.

"Let's just say I needed a change of scenery," Charlotte replied, her composure fraying at the edges. She'd had enough today—of the Harrisons, Thomas, and now this woman. "And you, Mrs. Wagner?" She couldn't suppress the curiosity that surged within her, nor the unease that knitted her brows together.

"Change of scenery," Isla repeated, a half-smile playing on her lips as she withdrew her hand from the flowers. "Yes, let's call it that."

The air between them grew thick with unspoken thoughts. Charlotte watched Isla's every move, a ballet of elegance and mystery.

"Is there anything else you'd like to know?" Charlotte asked, her tone cordial yet cautious.

"Plenty," Isla admitted, her gaze lingering on Charlotte's face for a moment longer than necessary before glancing around the foyer. "But perhaps another time. Thank you, Ms. Moore."

As Isla turned away, Charlotte found herself watching the retreating figure with a mix of suspicion and intrigue. Her gut told her that Isla's questions weren't mere pleasantries; they held purpose—though to what end, she couldn't fathom.

The grandfather clock in the corner of The Crown's lobby tolled five, its chimes resonating through the quiet expanse, a reminder that the day was waning. Charlotte glanced at its face, her fingers absentmindedly tracing the edge of the check-in counter, the wood worn smooth by years of greetings and farewells.

The front door opened again, and Amelia appeared once more.

"Mother, I'll just be upstairs," Amelia called out as she flew in, her voice disrupting the silence. She was already halfway up the grand staircase before Charlotte could even process her departure.

"Wait, Amelia—!" But it was too late; Amelia had vanished into the upper corridors, leaving behind a trail of floral perfume and unexplained urgency.

Charlotte sighed, her focus splintered.

"Focus, Charlotte," she murmured to herself, scanning the reservation list for the umpteenth time. It was all there—the names, dates, special requests—all meticulously recorded. Yet the words blurred together, her mind wandering back to Isla's veiled inquiries about her past in New York, about the inn's history, about Charlotte's own reasons for being here.

As the night descended, wrapping the inn in a shroud of dusk, Charlotte wondered if she, too, would emerge as steadfast as the old manor house—or if the mysteries harbored within these walls would prove too much for her.

CHAPTER SEVEN

Evening had settled like a soft shawl upon the old manor house, and the once grandiose dining room had transformed into a sanctuary of coziness, with flickering candles casting dancing shadows across the walls and soft lighting that glowed like amber fireflies caught in antique lamps.

Charlotte moved about the room with the grace of someone who knew every creak of the worn floorboards, every whisper of the sea breeze that slipped through the imperfect seal of the window frames. The table was dressed in her finest linen, creamy white and smooth beneath her fingertips as she smoothed out invisible wrinkles. She arranged the silverware with precision, forks and knives gleaming softly in the candlelight.

"Perfect," she murmured to herself, her voice a hushed note in the symphony of clinks and rustles. Her anticipation for the evening felt like effervescent bubbles in her chest.

"Mother, it looks lovely," Amelia's voice came from behind her, bringing a smile to Charlotte's face.

"Thank you, darling," Charlotte said, turning to beam at her daughter, feeling a swell of pride. "I wanted tonight to be special—for all of us. Simon is coming over for dinner again."

Her hands brushed over the back of a chair, the varnished wood smooth under her touch.

"Everything smells divine," Amelia added, leaning closer to sniff at the pot of stew bubbling on the stove.

"Let's hope it tastes just as good," Charlotte replied playfully, though internally she held a small flicker of doubt. It was silly, perhaps, but her desire to impress with her culinary skills was just another test of whether she truly belonged in Chesham.

Amelia grinned, her eyes sparkling with affection and mischief. "I have no doubt, Mother. You could make a gourmet meal out of seaweed and driftwood if you put your mind to it."

"Let's stick to the classics for now," Charlotte laughed, her worry easing as she glanced around the room one last time. Everything was set, each detail perfect. "We can even eat in the formal living room, by the fire, if everyone decides so. Hot chocolate after, and maybe a classic old Hollywood movie?"

Amelia's laughter echoed through The Crown. The young woman danced on the balls of her feet, an eager energy radiating from her as she glanced at the clock.

"Speaking of classics," Amelia began, her eyes alight with unspoken tales, "I might have to skip out on this masterpiece tonight, Mom."

"Skip out?" Charlotte quirked an eyebrow, half-amused, half-curious. She watched her daughter fidget, the mystery in her movements like a playful breeze that teased but never told its secrets.

"Sorry to spring it on you like this, but I'm meeting someone," Amelia confessed, coyly biting her lip. "A friend."

"Someone special?" Charlotte prodded gently, her heart warming at the thought of Amelia finding a friend in the village.

"Maybe," Amelia gave a noncommittal shrug, the enigmatic smile not quite reaching her lips. With a swift hug that caught Charlotte by surprise, Amelia whispered, "You deserve a good night too, you know." And just like that, she slipped away, leaving behind a trail of intrigue and a sputtering Charlotte, barely calling goodbye after before she was gone.

Left in the wake of her daughter's sudden departure, Charlotte turned to find Simon leaning against the doorframe in the open back door to the kitchen, an affectionate, knowing look in his ocean-blue eyes.

"Looks like we've been abandoned," Simon said, his voice a low thrum that resonated within the cozy confines of the inn.

"Seems so," Charlotte replied, her pulse quickening. She sauntered toward him. "What do you say we make the most of it?"

"Sounds like an excellent plan," he agreed, as he strode toward her with purposeful grace.

They shared a brief, warm kiss before parting, their foreheads brushing.

"Eat by the fire?"

"Sounds wonderful," he replied.

Their quiet laughter mingled with the crackle of the fireplace as they settled into the deep cushions of the sitting area, two souls orbiting closer in the intimacy of shared solitude. Charlotte found herself caught in the gravity of Simon's gaze, each flicker of candlelight reflecting in his eyes, weaving a silent conversation only they could understand. They savored their meal in occasional silence, punctuated by contented sighs and the occasional clatter of cutlery.

In the midst of their dinner, the doorbell rang—a delicate chime that seemed oddly intrusive. Charlotte's brows knitted together, a twinge of annoyance threading through her reverie.

"Excuse me for a moment," she said, smoothing her skirt as she rose from her seat.

"Of course," Simon replied, watching her go with a fondness that lingered in the air.

At the front desk, Isla stood, her presence like a cool breeze that threatened to disperse the warm atmosphere Charlotte had so carefully curated.

"Charlotte, I hate to be a bother, but could I trouble you for an extra pillow? And maybe a few more towels?" Isla asked, her voice lilting with an apologetic smile.

"Of course, Isla. I'll bring them to your room shortly," Charlotte assured her, the innkeeper's mask slipping seamlessly over her features.

"Thank you," Isla said, turning away, her silhouette momentarily caught in the glow of the hallway's nightlights.

Charlotte returned to the living room, her mind a whirlwind of thoughts. Would Isla's interruption derail the evening? She couldn't let it. Not when every second with Simon felt precious—a treasure she wasn't willing to squander.

"Everything okay?" Simon asked, concern etching his brow as Charlotte sat down again.

"Absolutely," she replied, her smile a little too practiced. "Just fulfilling the duties of an innkeeper."

"Your dedication is admirable," he said with a grin that reached his eyes. "But I feel a little possessive of you tonight."

Charlotte nodded, the warmth returning to her cheeks. "Oh? Well, I just need a minute…"

Charlotte excused herself with a grace that belied her racing pulse. She slipped out of the dining room, her feet whispering across the old wooden floorboards of The Crown Inn. The flickering candles cast long, dancing shadows behind her, their light waning just enough to shroud Simon in their warm embrace.

"Here," Charlotte muttered under her breath as she reached for the stack of plush towels and fluffed pillow, her hands steady despite the flutter in her chest. As she ascended the staircase, the wood creaked beneath her steps, a charming yet traitorous sound she had grown to love.

"Charlotte, dear, do you think I could also have a glass of that lovely lemon water you offered earlier?" Isla's voice floated down from the upper landing, as sweet and unexpected as a night-blooming jasmine.

"Of course!" Charlotte called back, her tone effortlessly cheerful. "I'll bring it up with the towels and pillow."

The stairs ended just shy of the corridor where Isla awaited, and Charlotte could hear Simon's voice filter through the air from below—a rich sound that seemed to resonate with the very foundations of the inn. But she couldn't make out what he'd said. She turned to see him stand, pushing his chair back with the intention of helping, no doubt.

Simon was by her side in moments. "You've been on your feet all evening. I'll grab the drink. Which cupboard?"

"Left side of the sink!" She replied quickly.

"Got it. Don't move. This is my domain now," Simon joked, and she heard the comforting sound of cabinet doors opening and closing.

Charlotte whisked away into the hall, finding Isla leaning against the doorframe of her room, her silhouette draped in the soft fabric of her nightgown, which caught the moonlight and gave her an ethereal glow.

"Here we are, towels fluffy enough for a queen and a pillow fit for a princess," Charlotte said with a flourish as she handed the items over.

"Thank you, my fairy godmother," Isla replied with a playful curtsy that made Charlotte chuckle. "But what about my midnight elixir?"

"Coming right up," Charlotte assured her, turning away just as Simon's footsteps signaled his ascent up the first few stairs.

"Wait!" Isla's voice halted Charlotte mid-step. "Could you also bring up some of those delightful shortbread cookies? They were divine."

"Divine?" Charlotte echoed, stalling. "Well, I suppose they did turn out rather well. I'll be back before you can say 'bibbidi-bobbidi-boo.'"

"Take your time," Isla said, unaware of the intricate dance unfolding around her. "I'm in no rush."

"Neither am I," Charlotte answered, a touch too quickly, her gaze darting to the top of the stairs where she saw Simon's shadow pause and retreat, the man himself evidently deciding to give them space.

She hastened back down, collecting the glass of lemon water from Simon with a whispered apology—and thanks—and a small plate of shortbread cookies. He gazed at her warmly and brushed her cheek with his lips, a promise and an enticement.

"Hurry back."

Her heart was a hummingbird in her chest, the thrill of near-misses adding an unexpected zest to the night.

"Here you go, lemon water to cleanse the palate and shortbread cookies to spoil it right after," Charlotte said with a twinkle in her eye as she presented the treats to Isla.

"You're spoiling me rotten," Isla laughed, accepting the offerings. "It's a good thing I don't stay here often, or I'd never leave."

"Consider it a perk of being our most charming guest," Charlotte replied, her smile lingering as she imagined Simon waiting below, wine bottle in hand, ready to pour them both another glass. "Goodnight, Isla," Charlotte said, her voice soft. She watched Isla disappear into her room and listened for the click of the latch before allowing herself a moment to lean against the cool wall, eyes closed, breathing deep.

"Everything okay?" Simon's voice startled her as she descended the last few steps, his presence like a beacon drawing her back to the world they had woven together.

"Better than okay," Charlotte assured him, her smile genuine now. "We have the night to ourselves, and I plan to make the most of it."

But the night seemed to have other plans.

"Charlotte, darling, could I trouble you for a fan? It's rather stuffy in my room," Isla called again from the top of the stairs, her voice as light and airy as the summer curtains fluttering in the parlor.

"Of course, let me just—" Charlotte began, glancing at Simon who was decanting a new bottle of rich red wine with deft movements, his rugged hands careful against the delicate crystal. "I'll be right back."

"Take your time," Simon said, his eyes holding a promise that wove through the air between them like silk.

Ascending the grand staircase, Charlotte located an electric fan from the guest amenities cupboard, her thoughts racing. How could she keep weaving this enchanting spell with Simon while attending to Isla's needs?

"Here you are," she said, presenting the fan to Isla with a smile that masked her internal juggling act.

"Thanks ever so much." Isla's gratitude felt plastic.

Returning to Simon, Charlotte allowed herself to be pulled back into their private cocoon. Their fingers brushed as she accepted her glass of wine, sending a shiver of anticipation down her spine.

"Where were we?" Charlotte whispered, her gaze locked with Simon's.

"Right about here," he replied, leaning in closer, his breath warm against her cheek.

"Charlotte, I hate to be a bother, but the bulb in my bedside lamp seems to have gone out," Isla's voice drifted down to them once again, cutting through the burgeoning intimacy like a ship's prow through calm waters.

"Of course, Isla," Charlotte responded, a hint of strain beginning to show in her otherwise serene facade. She turned to Simon with an apologetic look before slipping away once more.

In the solitude of the corridor, Charlotte fetched a new bulb, her mind churning. How many more interruptions before the spell was broken entirely? Returning to Isla, who was lounging in bed with the overhead room light blazing, Charlotte replaced the bulb with efficiency.

"Anything else you need?" Charlotte asked, hoping her words didn't betray the tension gripping her chest.

"No, that should be it. Thank you, Charlotte. You're a lifesaver."

Back downstairs, Simon looked up, his smile reigniting the warmth within her.

"You're very popular tonight," he murmured, drawing her close.

"Thank you, but I'm not exactly sure it's a good kind of popular," she replied, resting her head against his chest for a fleeting moment of peace.

"Charlotte, I'm sorry, I don't mean to interrupt," Isla's voice floated down once more, tinged with embarrassment. "But I seem to have left my glasses somewhere downstairs."

"Let me," Simon said, starting toward the stairs.

"Stay here," Charlotte instructed Simon, her tone laced with urgency. "I'll be quick."

As she moved to assist Isla, locating the glasses in the front foyer, Charlotte couldn't help but marvel at the absurdity of the situation. Here she was, orchestrating a ballet of near-misses, each step executed with the precision of a seasoned performer. Yet, with every pirouette, she grew more and more frustrated with the dance.

"Here they are," Charlotte handed the forgotten glasses to Isla, who offered a sheepish grin in return.

"Thank you, truly. Now, go enjoy your evening!"

"Goodnight, Isla," Charlotte said, though the repeated refrain felt like a wish hanging by a thread.

Descending the stairs, the sight of Simon waiting for her, patience etched into the lines of his face, was a balm to her frayed nerves.

"Sorry for all the interruptions," Charlotte said, her voice heavy with laughter and exasperation as she reclaimed her seat across from him.

"Nothing to apologize for," Simon reassured her, raising his glass. "To us, and to moments worth waiting for."

Their glasses chimed in agreement, the sound echoing through The Crown Inn like a vow. She watched Simon, who had stood up once more, ostensibly to stretch his legs but likely growing restless from the interminable string of interruptions.

"Nature calls," he said with an easy smile. "I'll be right back."

"Of course," Charlotte replied, her laugh a touch too high-pitched, betraying her inner turmoil. As he disappeared toward the restroom, she couldn't help but think how each absence felt like a reprieve and a curse all at once—a stolen moment to breathe, yet another chance for Isla to emerge.

Her thoughts were a whirlpool, spinning faster with every soft footstep she heard above. *If Isla steps out now, while Simon's away...* Fate seemed to favor the dramatic tonight. The floorboards creaked a warning overhead just as the restroom door clicked shut downstairs.

"Charlotte?" The voice floated down like a leaf on the wind, Isla's silhouette appearing at the top of the staircase.

"Coming!" Charlotte called. She ascended the stairs two at a time, a forced calm settling over her features as she greeted Isla with a practiced smile. "What can I help you with?"

"Would you happen to have a spare charger? My phone is nearly dead," Isla explained, her tone apologetic.

"Let me just check in the kitchen drawers," Charlotte said, already plotting her course to retrieve her own charger—she would deal without one for a night.

The humor of the situation was not lost on her—the universe playing its own game of hide and seek. She thought that the Harrisons would be the tough ones! But she procured the charger with a triumphant flourish.

"Here you are," Charlotte presented it to Isla, who took it with grateful hands.

"Thank you, Charlotte. You really do think of everything, don't you?" Isla remarked, unaware of the irony.

"Trying my best," Charlotte responded, her laughter genuine despite the undercurrent of stress.

"Goodnight, again," Isla said, the finality in her voice suggesting that this might indeed be the last request of the night.

"Sleep well," Charlotte replied, her relief palpable as she watched Isla retreat to her room and close the door with a soft click.

Descending the staircase once more, Charlotte's gaze lingered on the deserted hallway leading to the restrooms. And then there he was, reemerging into the dimly lit foyer area, his presence a beacon drawing her back into the sphere of their interrupted romance. His brow furrowed slightly as he caught sight of her, reading the subtle signs of her frazzled state.

"Everything alright?" Simon asked as she approached, his concern as endearing as it was unnecessary.

"Perfectly fine," Charlotte assured him, her voice steady as she reclaimed her seat. "All settled for the night, and we're free to enjoy what's left of ours."

"Sounds like a plan," Simon agreed, reaching across the table to gently squeeze her hand. "We've certainly earned a bit of peace."

Their fingers intertwined, and Charlotte allowed herself a deep, calming breath. With Isla's needs attended to and the night stretching before them like a blank canvas, Charlotte felt the anxiety ebb away— for now.

CHAPTER EIGHT

Dawn's tender light spilled through the mullioned windows of The Crown Inn's dining area the next morning, christening the mahogany tables and the terracotta tiles underfoot. Charlotte moved with quiet grace around the room, her thoughts as meticulously arranged as the cutlery before her. She had always believed that breakfast was more than just the first meal of the day; it was an artist's palette, an opportunity to paint the morning with flavors and colors.

"Good morning," she murmured, almost to herself, as she adjusted a vase of fresh daffodils, their yellow heads bobbing cheerfully at each table. Her fingers trailed over the petals gently. She placed a platter of sliced fruits next to a basket woven with an assortment of freshly baked bread. The scent of the pastries intertwined with the salty sea breeze that snuck in whenever the door swung open, bringing with it the promise of another day.

"Is the coffee Arabica or Robusta?" Mr. Harrison called out from the buffet line, peering over the steaming pots.

"Arabica, sourced from a small plantation in Colombia. It has a smoother flavor," Charlotte answered, her voice carrying the subtle pride of someone who valued the story behind each detail. In the way she presented the breakfast options, one could see the same care that had once gone into her canvases—each choice a stroke of intent. But the thought reminded her of how busy she'd been so far this summer, with little time to paint.

Mr. Harrison nodded, satisfied. As Charlotte adjusted a tray of cheeses, her mind drifted briefly to the life she'd left, where painting had been her only escape—here, every morning was a canvas awaiting her touch. She tucked a stray lock of hair behind her ear and checked the consistency of the porridge simmering on the stove, ensuring it was just right.

"Charlotte, do you have any of that splendid marmalade left?" asked another guest, his eyes hopeful.

"Of course, Mr. Bennett. I made extra this week," she replied, her lips curving into a smile that reached her eyes. She opened a cupboard and handed him a jar, the golden contents catching the sunlight, and watched as he spooned it onto his toast with relish.

Charlotte took a moment, leaning against the kitchen counter, to observe the guests as they filled their plates. Her heart swelled with a sense of accomplishment, seeing them savor the offerings she'd prepared. Each satisfied sigh and contented murmur was a balm to her nurturing spirit.

It was then that Isla Wagner pushed open the kitchen door, her entrance silent but for the soft click of the latch falling back into place. She stood framed by the doorway, a tall silhouette clad in a flowing dress that whispered of affluence and elegant indifference to the *quaintness* surrounding her. Her gaze, cool and observational, swept over the room before settling on Charlotte with a spark of curiosity.

"Good morning," Charlotte greeted, offering a smile as Isla approached the buffet. "I hope you find everything to your liking."

"Quite," Isla replied, her voice smooth, yet it carried an undercurrent of something more—a prying intent disguised as casual conversation. "You've done wonders with the place. It has an... authentic charm." She turned to face Charlotte, her eyes appraising the innkeeper standing amidst her culinary creations.

"Thank you," Charlotte said, feeling the weight of scrutiny but choosing to focus on the compliment. "I felt this old house deserved a chance to shine again."

"An artist from New York running a British B&B? That's quite a shift." Isla leaned against the table, plucking a grape from the fruit platter. "What made you leave the city for Chesham Cove?"

So she's read the website, Charlotte thought.

Charlotte paused, measuring her words with care. "Life can surprise you with unexpected turns," she admitted. "Sometimes, you have to follow where they lead, even if it brings you to the edge of the world."

"Why this edge?" Isla queried, a half-smile playing at the corner of her lips.

"Perhaps it was fate." Charlotte arranged the silverware with meticulous attention, creating a momentary barrier between herself and Isla's probing gaze. "Anyway, I believe there's beauty in new beginnings."

"Indeed." Isla's eyes narrowed slightly. "And do you plan to keep this... beauty all to yourself? What are your aspirations for The Crown?"

Charlotte glanced out the window, watching a seagull glide effortlessly on the sea breeze. "I want my guests to feel at home, even if they're miles away from theirs."

"Admirable," Isla conceded, her tone implying she understood more than she let on. "And does this vision have room for expansion? Or will you keep it as a well-kept secret?"

"Expansion isn't always synonymous with improvement," Charlotte countered gently, aware of the stakes such discussions held in a small community like Chesham Cove. Her thoughts went immediately to Thomas Windnell, and she had a sudden, horrifying thought—what if Isla was somehow a spy for the posh Brit? Sent to sabotage or gather intel for Windell? "I value intimacy and authenticity over grandeur. The inn is more than just a business; it's a personal investment."

"Personal..." Isla repeated softly, the word lingering between them like a shared secret. Her eyes seemed to hold a glimmer of respect—or was it merely a reflection of the sunlight?

Charlotte offered a plate of pastries to a—thankfully pleased—Mrs. Harrison, allowing the interaction to provide a natural pause in their conversation. She could feel Isla's persistent curiosity, but beneath the surface, there was also something akin to recognition—an understanding that journeys, no matter how different, often shared the same destination: a longing for purpose and a place to call home.

Isla's eyes wandered over the room before fixing back on Charlotte. "And has your daughter taken to this rustic life as well as you have?"

The question, innocuous as it might have seemed, sent a prickle of discomfort skittering down Charlotte's spine. She poured steaming coffee into a porcelain cup with practiced care to avoid betraying her unease. "Amelia is... embracing the change," she said cautiously, feeling the scrutiny like a spotlight. "She heads back across the pond to college soon."

How does Isla know Amelia is here?

"Embracing, hmm?" Isla's eyebrow arched, a silent prompt for more.

"Wholeheartedly," Charlotte insisted, even as her mind whispered doubts.

Before the conversation could delve deeper, the brisk patter of footsteps announced Amelia's serendipitous approach. The young woman appeared at the doorway, her hair pulled into a haphazard bun that suggested a hurried morning.

"Morning, Mum," Amelia chirped, snagging a piece of toast from a passing tray. Her eyes flickered to Isla, offering a polite nod before darting away. Amelia took a travel mug from a nearby cupboard and filled it with coffee.

"Off so soon?" Charlotte's voice held a note of concern, but she was careful to temper it with respect for her daughter's growing independence. Amelia had been out and about a lot over the past few days—and Charlotte's curiosity was piqued.

"Yep, online study group to prep for fall classes. Going to use the Chesham library," Amelia responded, already backing toward the exit. "Don't wait up!"

"Take a jacket, it'll be cold later," Charlotte called after her retreating figure, knowing full well the advice would go unheeded. A thought nagged at her—with the time difference, would there be a study group meeting now? Charlotte shook off the thought.

She turned back to Isla, finding the other woman's piercing gaze had softened somewhat. "She's finding her way," Charlotte added, more to herself than to Isla. It was a mantra she repeated often these days, a reassurance against the fluttering anxiety that came with letting go.

"Children do have a knack for that," Isla said, a hint of something unreadable in her tone. "I'm sure you've done well by her."

"Thank you," Charlotte replied, her heart giving an unexpected lurch of gratitude for the acknowledgment. She glanced around at the near-empty plates and contented murmurs of the other guests, allowing the rhythm of the inn to soothe her frayed nerves.

"Running this place—it's my anchor," she confessed, watching Isla absorb her words with an enigmatic smile.

"An anchor can be a lifeline... or it can hold you back," Isla mused cryptically, standing to leave. Charlotte thought about Simon's near-identical words at the pier, and something twisted in her stomach. Had Isla been listening in on them somehow, there?

"Perhaps," Charlotte acknowledged. "But for now, it's exactly where I need to be."

As Isla exited with a curt nod but no reply, the click of the kitchen door latch echoed in the stillness, leaving Charlotte with a sense of disquiet. The other guests filtered out, and as Charlotte busied herself with clearing the tables, her thoughts lingered on the fine line between anchoring oneself and being dragged down.

What was Charlotte setting herself up for?

CHAPTER NINE

That afternoon, Charlotte stood on a rickety wooden ladder in the ballroom of The Crown Inn, squinting up at the elaborate crystal chandelier that hung from the high ceiling. She had noticed one of the lightbulbs was out and had eagerly grabbed the ladder, thinking it would be a quick and easy fix. But as soon as she unscrewed the burnt-out bulb, the fixture let out an ominous creak and shifted slightly.

"Oh no, no, no," Charlotte muttered, grimacing as she tried to steady the giant light. It wobbled precariously, the crystals jangling against each other in a cacophony of clinks and clanks. She stretched her arm upward, fingers straining, but only succeeded in bumping the chandelier again, sending it swaying wildly.

Charlotte clung to the ladder, eyes widening in panic. "Stop! Stop moving!" she yelled at the light fixture, as if it could obey her command. The chandelier continued its erratic dance, crystals tinkling in protest. Charlotte lunged upward one last time, finally grasping the metal frame.

"Gotcha!" She declared in triumph. But her victory was short-lived. With a piercing crack, the ancient ceiling hook holding the chandelier gave way. Charlotte barely had time to gasp and let go before the giant light came crashing down. She cringed, waiting for the sound of shattering crystal.

Instead, the chandelier landed with a heavy thud in the center of a large Persian rug that spanned the lobby floor. Charlotte slowly opened one eye. The rug had cushioned the fall, leaving the chandelier intact. Letting out a sigh of relief, Charlotte scrambled down the ladder.

"Well, that could have been a disaster," she said with a nervous laugh, standing over the heap of crystal and brass. She placed her hands on her hips, blowing a loose strand of hair out of her eyes as she surveyed the mess she had made.

So much for a quick fix.

Charlotte surveyed the tangle of chandelier and rug, hands on her hips and a defeated sigh escaping her lips. She had been so sure she could handle this minor repair on her own, eager to surprise Amelia with the completed project when she arrived home later that day.

Amelia. Charlotte glanced at her watch, realizing her daughter should be pulling up any minute now. They had planned today to tackle the first round of small house fixes together, excited by the prospect of revitalizing the old inn as a mother-daughter endeavor. Surely, he study group wouldn't take very long. It had been hours already.

Charlotte pictured the eager smile that would light up Amelia's face when she saw the improvements underway, the joy of rolling up their sleeves together to restore the charm and beauty of this place. She could already envision Amelia's clever suggestions, her artistic eye for detail. They worked so well as a team.

The sound of tires crunching on gravel snapped Charlotte from her reverie. She hurried to the front window just in time to see her daughter's taxi pull into the driveway.

"Mom, I'm here!" Amelia's voice rang out as the front door swung open. "Ready to get started on Operation Crown Inn!"

When Amelia burst into the ballroom, Charlotte turned a strained smile on her face. "Amelia! Hi, sweetie..."

Charlotte's voice trailed off as Amelia stepped inside and surveyed the scene before her. The young woman's eyebrows shot up as she took in the debris, tools strewn about, and half-painted walls.

"Whoa, looks like you really went for it, Mom," Amelia said with an amused grin.

Charlotte gave a weak chuckle, pushing a strand of hair off her sweaty, dusty forehead. "I, uh, got a little carried away trying to get things started before you arrived."

"A little carried away?" Amelia teased. "It looks like a tornado hit this place!"

Charlotte sighed, her shoulders slumping. "I know, I'm sorry. I wanted to make some progress as a surprise, but I just made a huge mess instead."

Amelia set her bag down and put a reassuring hand on her mother's arm. "Hey, it's okay. This is why we're doing this together, right? What matters is that we're both here now, ready to fix this place up."

Charlotte smiled gratefully at her daughter's optimism. Maybe this renovation disaster could still turn into something good.

"You're right," she said. "Now, let's get to work cleaning up my mess before we do any more demolition. I clearly need your help!"

Amelia playfully tossed her a broom. "Roger that! Operation Crown Inn: Phase One - Clean Up Mom's Chaos!"

Together, they laughed and started tackling the debris. Charlotte wiped her brow, smearing a streak of dust across her forehead. Her hair was matted with sweat, strands falling haphazardly from her ponytail. She glanced down at her ripped jeans and dirt-smudged shirt, sighing at the utter disarray of her appearance. This was not how she had envisioned the day.

The sound of the ballroom door opening drew Charlotte's attention. She turned, surprised to see Isla entering the room. Charlotte felt a flush of embarrassment, acutely aware of her own unkempt state.

"Oh! Hello," Charlotte said, quickly trying to smooth her hair.

Isla paused, taking in the debris and Charlotte's flustered demeanor. "I hope I'm not intruding. The door was unlocked, so I let myself in."

"No, not at all!" Charlotte said hastily. She attempted a nonchalant laugh. "As you can see, I'm just working on some, uh, renovations."

Isla nodded, glancing around the wreckage. "It looks like quite the project. Is everything alright?"

Charlotte cringed inwardly. This was not the polished impression she had intended to make on Isla. But she straightened her shoulders and met Isla's gaze.

"Everything's under control," she said, hoping she sounded more confident than she felt. "Just a few minor setbacks, that's all."

Isla smiled kindly. "Of course. Well, please let me know if I can help with anything."

Charlotte gestured to the exposed wiring dangling from the ceiling. "I was trying to replace this light fixture and things got a bit...out of hand." She shook her head ruefully. "I thought I could handle it on my own but clearly electrical work is not my forte."

Isla tilted her head, examining the precarious setup. "Electrical can be tricky if you don't know what you're doing. It looks like you gave it a good effort though."

Charlotte laughed. "That's one way to put it. The truth is I had no idea what I was getting into."

She swept a hand over her disheveled appearance. "As you can probably tell from the state I'm in."

Isla smiled warmly. "You should see some of my DIY projects. I once demoed my entire kitchen only to realize I had no idea how to install the new cabinets."

Charlotte felt herself relaxing. "Oh no! What did you do?"

"Let's just say we ate a lot of takeout that week while I figured it out," Isla said with a grin.

Charlotte chuckled, appreciating Isla's effort to commiserate and put her at ease. She found herself wanting to make a good impression on this woman. She almost asked—*we?* at Isla's confession, wondering if the woman was married, but held back. Perhaps Isla wasn't a spy for Windnell, but a woman mid-divorce, as Charlotte had been.

Gathering her composure, Charlotte said, "Well, I won't keep you. But thank you for the empathy. Maybe I'll take you up on the offer for help soon."

Isla nodded. "Of course."

Charlotte smiled as Isla walked away, and then looked around at the mess she'd made, shaking her head and laughing softly. "Alright, let's try this again," she muttered.

Taking a deep breath, she went to find a broom. The inn wasn't going to renovate itself, after all. And now, she felt motivated to tackle it one step at a time. Charlotte swept up the debris with renewed energy, making a mental list of tasks for the day. She'd start simple - clearing up this mess, checking for any electrical hazards. As she swept up the last of the debris and leaned the broom against the wall, she stood in the center of the room, surveying the damage. The exposed wiring still sparked intermittently, and the hole in the ceiling let in a draft.

It wasn't exactly the vision she'd had. Charlotte sighed, pushing a strand of hair off her sweaty forehead. The work ahead seemed daunting. First things first - she needed to call an electrician before she could fix the ceiling.

"Honey, you want to finish up the painting on the far wall? I have to go make a call."

Amelia nodded.

In her office a moment later, Charlotte took a deep breath as she dialed the number for the electrician. She knew first impressions mattered, and she wanted to come across as calm and collected on the phone.

"Hi, I'm Charlotte Moore, the new owner of the Old Crown Inn," she began, hoping her voice sounded steadier than she felt. "Unfortunately, I've run into a bit of a wiring issue that I could use some help with."

She went on to describe the problem - the short circuit, the sparks, the fallen light fixture. The electrician assured her he could come take a look that afternoon.

Charlotte hung up, feeling relieved. One step down. Now to make herself presentable before he arrived. She looked down at her disheveled appearance and had to laugh. Dirt smeared her cheeks, sawdust sprinkled her hair. Her clothes were rumpled and sweat-stained. Isla had caught her at her absolute worst.

Recalling Isla's poise and elegance in contrast to her own frantic state made Charlotte's cheeks burn. She couldn't imagine what Isla must think of the American who fancied herself an innkeeper.

But Isla had been gracious, not judgmental. She'd even offered to help, as if she saw past the surface mess to something deeper in Charlotte. That small act of kindness buoyed Charlotte's spirit.

Sometimes cold and distant, calculating, and sometimes warm and friendly—Charlotte couldn't quite read the tall, lithe woman. What was Isla's secret? And did it have to do with her own past—or the future of something that Charlotte herself held dear?

CHAPTER TEN

Charlotte arrived at the harbor a few hours later, the salty sea air filling her lungs. She spotted Simon on the dock, hunched over a pile of nets. His sleeves were rolled up, revealing tanned, muscular arms that glistened with sweat in the afternoon sun.

"You're hard at work today," Charlotte said, coming up behind him.

Simon jumped, startled by her sudden appearance. "Charlotte! I didn't hear you." He flashed her a grin, his green eyes crinkling at the corners. "I'm just tinkering with some new net designs. I think they'll help bring in bigger hauls."

Charlotte studied the intricate knots and weaves. She admired his passion for innovating. His mind was always working.

"It's looking great," she said, squeezing his shoulder. A touch that said both 'I miss you' and 'I'm proud of you.'

"Thanks." Simon wiped his brow, smearing a streak of grime across his forehead. "I got caught up in it and lost track of time. Have you been waiting long?"

"No, I just got here."

They shared a smile, content just to be together. The harbor lapped gently against the hulls of the boats, a soothing rhythm.

"Should we go grab an early supper?" Simon asked.

Charlotte nodded, linking her arm through his. His skin smelled of the sea. "I'm starving. Amelia and I repainted the whole ballroom today, and we had an electrician rewire and rehang the old chandelier." She left out the part where it had come crashing down, *Phantom of the Opera-style.*

"Good work," he said. "And hard. No wonder you're hungry."

Charlotte and Simon strolled arm-in-arm along the harbor toward their favorite cafe. The sunshine warmed Charlotte's face, and the salty breeze tousled her hair. Her happy bubble was burst by the sudden ringing of her phone. She fished it out of her bag, seeing Sally's name flash on the screen. Sally, who worked at the bakery see,med to know everyone's business.

"Sorry, I should take this. It's Sally," she said apologetically.

Simon nodded. "Of course, go ahead."

Charlotte answered the call. "Hi Sally, what's up?"

Sally's bubbly voice came through the line. "Charlotte, honey, I think someone just saw your father! He came into the bakery and ordered a coffee and croissant. I didn't get a chance to talk to him, but I could swear it was him. The counter girl described him to a tee."

Charlotte froze, nearly dropping the phone. Her father? Here in Chesham Cove? It wasn't possible. Was it?

She stammered into the phone, "A-are you sure Sally? I mean, it's been so long..."

"I know it seems crazy, but I really think it was him!" Sally said excitedly. "You should come to the bakery right away in case he comes back."

Charlotte's mind was reeling. After all these years, could her father really have just shown up out of the blue? She murmured distractedly into the phone, "Okay...I'll be right there."

Hanging up, she turned to Simon, knowing her shock and confusion must be written all over her face.

Simon noticed Charlotte's stunned expression as she ended the call. "Is everything okay?" he asked gently.

She blinked a few times, as if coming out of a daze. "I'm...I'm not sure," she said haltingly.

Simon furrowed his brow in concern. "What is it? What's happened?"

Charlotte took a shaky breath, still processing the news. "That was Sally from the bakery. She says she just saw my father there."

"Your father?" Simon repeated in surprise. He'd been privy to Charlotte's search for the man, though there had been little to share recently.

Charlotte nodded, her eyes distant. "I haven't seen or heard from him in so many years. Not since..." Her voice trailed off.

Simon gave her hand a supportive squeeze. "I can't imagine how shocking this must be for you."

Charlotte turned her palm up and clutched his hand tightly, as if drawing strength from his solid grasp. "I just don't understand. Why now, after all this time?"

Simon searched her face with compassion. "Do you need to go? I can meet up with you later, once you've had a chance to process this."

Charlotte nodded, not letting go of his hand. "I will. Thank you, Simon." With a final supportive squeeze, she released his hand and hurried off, her mind swirling with questions about the sudden reappearance of Henry.

Charlotte hurried along the harbor, her heels clicking against the weathered boards of the pier. Despite the summer heat, she felt chilled, questions swirling through her mind.

Why was her father here after all these years? Would he be shocked to see her? Charlotte had tried for so long to move past the pain of his abandonment, and his unexpected return threatened to reopen those old wounds.

She drew in a shaky breath as she approached the bakery, Sally's lilting voice drifting through the open door as she chatted with a customer. Charlotte steeled her nerves and stepped inside. The scent of freshly baked bread enveloped her, but she barely noticed, scanning the cozy shop for any sign of the man she once called Father. But he was nowhere to be seen.

"Oh, Charlotte dear!" Sally bustled over, face alight with excitement. "You just missed him. Your father was here not fifteen minutes ago."

"Are you sure?"

"Yep!" Sally affirmed, nodding vigorously. "Rumor is he's been seen chatting up folks over by the harbor and asking about The Crown, too. Quite the mysterious figure, if you ask me."

Charlotte's mind raced with images of her estranged father, a man whose features had blurred with time in her memory. The possibility of his proximity sent a jolt of adrenaline through her. She could almost picture him there, standing against the backdrop of Chesham Cove's rugged cliffs, a living ghost from her past.

Charlotte's heart sank. "Did he say where he was going?"

Sally shook her head, wispy gray curls bouncing. "No, afraid not. But he can't have gone far. I'm sure if you ask around town, someone will know where to find him. Agnes, maybe?"

Charlotte nodded, thanking Sally absently as she turned to leave. Back out on the pier, she pulled out her phone to text Simon.

"He's gone again. But I'm going to search the town to see if I can find him."

Simon's response came quickly. "I'm here if you need me. We'll get through this together."

Despite everything, his words brought a hint of a smile to her lips. With Simon by her side, she could face whatever was coming next.

Charlotte sent a text to her Cousin Agnes to check if Henry had come there, and then pocketed her phone and headed into town, hope and trepidation warring within her. Old Tom at the pub thought he had seen a man headed toward the cliffs.

"Plaid scarf. Light jacket, navy I think," Tom said.

Charlotte hurried in that direction, the wind whipping her hair as she climbed higher. At the top, she spotted a lone figure gazing out to sea. Plaid scarf. Navy jacket. Heart pounding, she approached slowly. "Dad?"

The man turned, and Charlotte gasped. It wasn't her father, after all, just a random tourist. The crushing disappointment nearly staggered her.

She blinked back tears as she pulled out her phone again. "False alarm," she texted Simon. "It wasn't him."

His reply was swift. "I'm so sorry. Come back to the harbor when you're ready. I'll be here waiting for you."

Charlotte took a shaky breath, casting one last glance over the sea. She had been so sure this time. With a heavy heart, she turned and headed back down the cliffs. At least Simon would be there, a comforting constant amidst the chaos.

As Charlotte made her way back down from the cliffs, the weight of disappointment heavy in her chest, her phone vibrated. She pulled it out, seeing a call from Agnes. Her heart leapt with a mix of hope and anxiety. She answered quickly, "Agnes, hi. Have you seen him? Is Henry with you?"

There was a pause on the other end, and then Agnes' voice, tinged with concern. "No, Charlotte, I'm sorry. There's been no sign of him here. I've been asking around, but nobody seems to know anything. Are you okay?"

Charlotte felt a lump form in her throat. This was just another dead end, another moment of hope dashed. "I thought... I thought I saw him just now," she confessed, her voice barely more than a whisper. "But it was a mistake. Just a tourist."

Agnes sighed sympathetically. "I'm so sorry, Charlotte."

Everyone keeps saying that, Charlotte thought. *But no one really understands.*

"Thanks, Agnes. I'll keep looking." Charlotte ended the call, feeling a profound sense of loneliness envelop her. The tourist's mistake, coupled with the lack of news from Agnes, left her feeling more lost than ever.

Charlotte suddenly wanted to talk to her sister, but the time difference—Roxanne wouldn't likely pick up. She texted her anyway, asking to talk. She needed to hear the voice of the one person who would truly understand.

She stood there for a moment, trying to gather her strength, the sounds of the sea and the cries of the seagulls a distant background to her troubled thoughts. Her father's absence, the unresolved questions, and now this fruitless chase – it all seemed too much to bear.

With a heavy heart, she began her walk back to the harbor, to Simon. He would be there, waiting, ready to offer comfort and support. But even the thought of his steadying presence couldn't dispel the sadness that clung to her like a shadow.

CHAPTER ELEVEN

Charlotte headed home in the darkening evening after spending an hour or so with Simon. Chesham Cove sprawled out before her like an open book, each person a sentence, every building a paragraph—but Charlotte felt unfinished, a rough draft. But somewhere within these pages might be the answer to the question that had suddenly reignited within her heart.

Her boots clicked a steady rhythm on the cobblestones as she made her way through the familiar maze of streets. With each step, anticipation coiled tighter inside her chest, a mix of hope and trepidation knitting together.

"Could it really have been him?" The thought kept pace with her strides. It was ludicrous, the idea that her estranged father would appear here, of all places. Yet, the universe had a sense of humor, placing her at the edge of the world she once knew, only to tease her with echoes of her past.

She passed by shop windows reflecting a woman who looked composed, yet her pulse fluttered like a caged bird, eager for the freedom of answers. Charlotte tucked a stray auburn curl behind her ear, a small gesture of fortitude.

As Charlotte continued her walk, the evening air crisp and cool around her, the quaint charm of Chesham Cove took on a different hue in the fading light. The street lamps cast a soft glow, painting the cobbled streets in a warm, inviting light. Despite the beauty, Charlotte's mind remained preoccupied, wrestling with the possibility of her father's presence in this small corner of the world.

Turning a corner, she paused, her breath catching in her throat. There, ahead of her, stood a man in a plaid scarf and navy coat, distinctly different from the tourist she had mistaken earlier on the cliffs. This man's posture, the way he stood gazing into a shop window, the set of his shoulders - it all struck a chord in Charlotte's memory.

Her heart pounded in her chest as she stood frozen, observing him. Could this really be her father? The distance between them felt like a chasm filled with years of absence and unanswered questions. She took a tentative step forward, her mind a whirlwind of emotions.

The man turned slightly, and for a brief moment, their eyes met. Charlotte's heart skipped a beat. There was something familiar in that glance, a fleeting connection that tugged at her heartstrings. The man's face was partially obscured by the shadows, making it hard to discern his features clearly.

Compelled by a mixture of hope and fear, Charlotte moved closer, her steps hesitant. As she approached, the man turned away, continuing down the street. Charlotte quickened her pace, not wanting to lose sight of him, her mind racing with questions. Was this a mere coincidence, or had fate brought her face to face with her past?

She trailed behind the man at a discreet distance, her gaze locked on his broad shoulders as they moved with an air of casual certainty. He navigated Chesham Cove's cobbled streets with ease, as though he knew every brick and crack by heart. She kept herself half-hidden behind clusters of chatting tourists and locals still bustling about the evening streets, using them as a living screen to mask her presence.

"Hey-o!" the man called out, his voice carrying over the hum of the crowd.

"Hello, stranger! How goes it?" replied an elderly gentleman from his perch outside the barbershop, newspaper in hand.

"It's going well, thanks."

Charlotte watched the exchange, her heart tapping a staccato rhythm against her ribs. Each word from the man's mouth was like a drop of rain on the parched soil of her curiosity. The sound of his voice, warm and affable, was not quite how she remembered her father's, but then again, memories could be deceitful, especially those marinated in time.

She quickened her pace as the man turned down a narrow lane.

"Stay back, stay quiet," she coached herself, a mantra to keep her steps careful and her breath even. The man had become the axis on which her world currently spun, each rotation feeding her anticipation, stretching it thin. Charlotte tucked another unruly strand of hair behind her ear, a nervous tic she barely noticed anymore. She pressed on, driven by the fragile hope that this stranger might hold the key to a door long closed in her heart.

"Please," she whispered to no one, "let this not be another dead end."

The shadow of the church steeple stretched long across the cobblestone as Charlotte followed the stranger into the quiet solace of St. Mary's graveyard. The man paused by a weathered tombstone, tracing the name etched upon it with a tender finger. Charlotte held her breath, waiting, watching from behind an ancient yew tree, its branches a haven for whispered secrets.

"Geraldine," the man spoke softly, his voice carrying in the still air, "my love, bet you're having a laugh up there."

Charlotte's heart plummeted—her mother's name was not Geraldine. Her stomach knotted with the sharp twinge of disappointment; she had been wrong. With a heavy sigh, she stepped out from her hiding place, her presence an unspoken apology to the somber tranquility she'd disturbed.

"Excuse me," she called out, her voice unsteady, betraying her dashed hopes.

The man turned, a gentle confusion in his eyes. "Yes, miss? Can I help you?"

"I—I thought you were someone else," Charlotte admitted, tucking a strand of hair behind her ear, her gaze flickering away. "I'm sorry for intruding."

"No harm done," he replied with a disarming smile. "Easy to mistake a face sometimes, especially in a town like this." He tipped his hat and wandered off, leaving Charlotte alone with the stone angels and her own crestfallen thoughts.

"Where are you, Dad?" she murmured, more to herself than the departed souls around her. She took a moment to compose herself, and as she exited the graveyard, Charlotte's steps led her unwittingly past the picture windows of The Crested Wave, a quaint establishment nestled between a jewelry store and a flower store. Inside, amid the clinking of cups and the murmur of conversation, sat Amelia and Nathan—Sally's twenty-something son—their heads bent close over shared laughter.

They didn't see Charlotte; they were too enveloped in each other's company, a cocoon of youthful affection. Charlotte's feet rooted to the spot, watching the tableau—a snapshot of innocent romance backdropped by the soft glow of fairy lights and steam rising from mugs of hot cocoa.

For a heartbeat, she considered tapping on the glass, announcing her presence, but something held her back. It was a delicate thing, this burgeoning relationship before her, and she knew better than to rush in clumsily. Instead, Charlotte watched, a silent witness to this new chapter unfolding in her daughter's life.

Amelia looks happy, Charlotte thought, the warmth from the scene seeping into her chilled bones. With a deep breath, Charlotte turned away from the café, a faint smile playing on her lips. It was remarkable, watching Amelia like this—so grown-up, so at ease.

"Mom?" A voice broke through her reverie, and Charlotte jumped guiltily, but it was only a passerby on their phone, oblivious to the depth of Charlotte's internal conflict.

The joy in Amelia's eyes was unmistakable, and it filled Charlotte with a sense of triumph—it was a mother's victory to see her child happy. Yet, there lurked a shadow of frustration; why hadn't Amelia confided in her? She had been playing coy all this time. The thought stung sharper than the chill in the air. Here she was, an outsider to her daughter's life. The realization pinched, but Charlotte knew that to intervene now would be to undermine the very independence she had always encouraged.

Her footsteps echoed on the cobblestones as she paced lightly, wrestling with emotions that tugged in opposite directions. "She's finding her way," Charlotte reasoned, trying to anchor herself in understanding. "Isn't that what I taught her to do?"

But the protective instinct, honed over two decades of motherhood, did not easily relent. Charlotte's hands fidgeted with the hem of her scarf, the woolen fabric slipping through her fingers like the sands of time—Amelia's childhood, slipping away.

"Hi there, are you okay?" The concerned inquiry came from a shopkeeper standing at the entrance of his store, eyeing Charlotte curiously.

"Never better," she replied with a tight smile, her facade uncracked, though her heart was anything but serene. Turning back to the window, she watched as Amelia leaned into Nathan, her head resting against his shoulder in a picture of contentment. Charlotte offered one last glance through the window, then stepped away, her boots crunching softly on the cobblestone path. With each step, she practiced releasing a little more of the tether, allowing space for Amelia.

The cobblestone streets of Chesham Cove lay silent beneath the hush of twilight, and Charlotte found herself alone with her thoughts, the echo of her footsteps as thunderous as her thoughts. The soft glow from the street lamps cast long shadows that danced alongside her, mirroring the tumult of emotions that had held her captive just moments ago.

Charlotte's mind was a labyrinth as she walked home, each step taking her deeper into a maze of confusion and worry. The possibility of her father being in town, a man she hadn't seen in years, loomed over her like a dark cloud. Every stranger in a plaid scarf and navy coat became a potential sighting, a glimmer of hope that quickly fizzled out, leaving her more disheartened.

Then there was Amelia, who seemed to be drifting further away into her own world, a world where Charlotte felt like an outsider looking in. The sight of Amelia with Nathan, so engrossed in each other, was both a comfort and a pang of loneliness. Why hadn't Amelia told her about him? Was their relationship changing, leaving Charlotte on the fringes?

And Isla's secret, still unknown, added another layer of mystery and unease. What was she hiding? How did it all connect to the tangled web of events unfolding in Chesham Cove?

With each thought, Charlotte's heart grew heavier, the burden of unanswered questions and unresolved emotions weighing on her. The quaint charm of the town seemed distant now, overshadowed by the personal turmoil she was experiencing.

Finally reaching The Crown, she let out a weary sigh, the familiar façade of the inn offering little solace tonight. She made her way to her room, the silence of the inn a blessing. Falling into bed, Charlotte lay there, her mind racing with increasingly confused thoughts. The puzzle pieces of her life in Chesham Cove were scattered, and she felt no closer to putting them together. As exhaustion finally overtook her, Charlotte drifted into a restless sleep, her dreams a jumble of faces and whispers and empty, dark alleyways.

CHAPTER TWELVE

The next morning, as usual, Charlotte glided through the dining room, a serene smile on her face as she refilled coffee cups and asked after her guests.

"More bacon?" she offered warmly to the elderly man reading a newspaper. He gave her a grateful nod, and she piled more crispy strips onto his plate.

She felt a deep sense of pride as she looked around at the happy patrons chatting over steaming mugs and hearty breakfasts. When she had first arrived in Chesham Cove, The Old Crown Inn had been dusty and neglected, with peeling wallpaper and cobwebs in every corner. But in the last few months, with relentless hard work, she had transformed the old manor. She focused on that accomplishment—and the mental list of things she had to do today—to distract her from reflecting on the previous day's emotional low.

After clearing empty plates and bidding her guests a good morning, Charlotte moved through the cozy front sitting room straightening pillows and plumping cushions. She paused to add another log to the crackling fire, letting its warmth and light fill her spirit. As she wiped down side tables and arranged fresh flowers, her movements flowed gracefully like a dance, sweeping away the greys and blacks of her past.

Charlotte hummed softly to herself as she tidied up the sitting room. As she fluffed the pillows on the overstuffed sofa, her eyes drifted to the large bay window overlooking the gardens. Movement outside caught her attention. She paused her cleaning and stepped closer to the window, peering out curiously.

There was a figure moving furtively amongst the hedgerows, partially obscured by the fountain. Charlotte leaned forward, brows furrowed. Who was lurking out there? The form appeared masculine, though she couldn't quite make out any distinguishing features at this distance.

Feeling a flutter of apprehension in her stomach, Charlotte set aside her cleaning rag. She had to find out who this stranger was and what he was doing sneaking around the grounds. Smoothing her apron, she headed briskly to the front door and stepped outside into the crisp morning air. The gravel path crunched softly under her shoes as she made her way around the side of the inn toward the gardens.

As she drew nearer, Charlotte slowed her pace, moving cautiously now. She didn't want to startle the intruder. Heart pounding, she peered around a large rhododendron bush, finally getting a clear view of the man. He had his back to her and seemed to be intently watching the inn. Charlotte took a deep breath. It was time to find out what he was up to.

Charlotte took a step forward, gravel crunching under her shoes. The man spun around, eyes wide.

"Simon?" Charlotte blurted in surprise.

Simon stood there looking caught off guard, a faint blush rising on his cheeks.

"Oh, Charlotte, I uh..." He stammered, clearly flustered at being discovered.

Charlotte frowned, feeling confused and a bit hurt. What was Simon doing sneaking around her inn? Here he was, acting like a trespasser.

"What are you doing here?" She asked, unable to keep the accusation out of her tone.

Simon ran a hand through his hair. "I'm sorry, I didn't mean to startle you. I just wanted to see..." He trailed off as the sound of crunching gravel signaled a new arrival.

Charlotte turned to see Isla approaching from the other direction. The woman slowed as she spotted Charlotte, looking at her questioningly.

Charlotte's eyes darted to Simon, who was now behind a nearby bush. She felt a knot forming in her stomach. Charlotte stared after him in surprise. Why was he hiding? What was Isla's connection to Simon?

Isla smiled, waved, and went into the inn.

Charlotte let out a breath, even more perplexed. As she watched Isla disappear inside, Simon emerged cautiously from the bushes. Clearly, he had some explaining to do.

Charlotte turned to Simon with a bewildered look. "What on earth is going on? Why were you hiding in the bushes from Isla?"

Simon ran a hand through his hair and sighed. "It's complicated. Isla is...my ex-wife."

"Your *ex-wife?*" Charlotte repeated in shock.

"Yes. We've been separated for years, though not formally divorced yet," he explained. "I saw her in town yesterday, and I remembered your annoying, needy guest from the other night, and I connected the two. So I came to see what she was doing here."

Charlotte's mind raced, trying to make sense of this new information. Isla's probing questions suddenly seemed less innocuous. And Simon—well, to say that she was hurt over his sneaking and hiding was a bit of an understatement. Suddenly, her old insecurities about the two of them reared their heads. And, she thought, with good reason. Her voice was cold when she spoke.

"But why is she staying at my inn?" Charlotte asked. "Does she know about...us?"

Simon shook his head. "I don't think so. She's probably here to finalize the divorce paperwork. Though with Isla, I can never be sure."

He gazed up at the windows of the inn, his expression unreadable. Charlotte felt a pang of jealousy flare up despite her attempts to keep herself even. Clearly, there was still a lot of history between them.

"I should get back to work," Charlotte murmured, feeling suddenly deflated. The encounter with Isla had shifted something intangibly. Charlotte wasn't sure where she and Simon stood anymore, but a shadow of uncertainty had been cast over their deepening bond.

Charlotte took a deep breath to steady her nerves before turning back to Simon.

"I appreciate you telling me the truth," she said. "But I have to admit, I'm feeling a bit shaken up by all of this. I thought we were building something meaningful here."

Simon stepped closer and took her hands in his. "We are," he said earnestly. "Nothing has changed between us just because Isla showed up. The past is the past."

Her father leapt into her mind. *The past is the past?*

Charlotte searched his eyes, wanting to believe him but still plagued by doubts. "It's not that simple though, is it? You have a history with her that I'll never fully understand. And you didn't tell me she was here!"

"A history I'm trying to put behind me," Simon insisted. "You're the one I want to move forward with. And, Charlotte, I—I wasn't trying to deceive you. I'm as shocked as you are."

He gently tucked a strand of hair behind Charlotte's ear. She felt her pulse quicken being so close to him.

"Please don't let Isla's presence here undermine what we have," he implored. "This thing between us - it's real."

Charlotte nodded slowly. She knew in her heart he was speaking the truth. She wouldn't let her insecurities sabotage their chance at happiness.

"You're right," she said finally. "I'm sorry for doubting you. It's just...it's been a long time since I've let someone in."

Simon smiled, visibly relieved. "I know."

He pulled her close, and she rested her head on his chest, taking comfort in the steadiness of his heartbeat. Charlotte wanted to believe Simon's reassuring words, but a nagging doubt still lingered in the back of her mind. As much as she tried to push it away, she couldn't ignore the questions swirling through her thoughts. Charlotte lifted her head from Simon's chest and took a step back, folding her arms across herself protectively.

"I care about you, I really do," she began hesitantly. "But I need you to be honest with me. Is there more going on with Isla that you haven't told me?"

Simon sighed and ran a hand through his windswept hair. "I should have known this wasn't going to be easy," he muttered, almost to himself.

Looking Charlotte in the eyes, Simon continued gently, "You're right that there's more to it. Isla didn't just show up out of the blue. We've been in contact again recently."

Charlotte inhaled sharply but remained silent, waiting for him to explain further.

"She asked to give things another try between us," Simon confessed. "But I was very clear that my heart lies with you now." He took Charlotte's hands in his own. "You have to believe me, there is nothing left between Isla and I. Seeing her here only confirmed that for me."

Charlotte searched his earnest face. She could see the truth in his words. Nodding slowly, she squeezed his hands.

"Okay," she said simply. "I believe you."

The relief on Simon's face was evident. He drew her close once more. Charlotte rested her head on his shoulder once more, but she was far from placated. Isla had come just to sign divorce papers after all this time? Her arrival seemed too coincidental, too perfectly timed, just as things between Charlotte and Simon were progressing.

Why was Isla really here?

CHAPTER THIRTEEN

Charlotte stood at the window in the ballroom, gazing out at the rocky coastline bathed in morning light. The waves crashed and foamed against the cliffs, the sound both soothing and sorrowful—and the turmoil of the water mirrored her own inner tumult. She had set up her easel and paints, but she was having trouble really getting into the landscape she was painting. Charlotte started when she heard the door open behind her.

Charlotte turned to see her Amelia breeze into the room, cheeks flushed.

"Oh, hi, Mom," Amelia said. "I was looking for you. I'm heading into town to meet up with some friends."

Charlotte opened her mouth to ask who exactly these "friends" were, but stopped herself.

Nathan.

Amelia was an adult now, she reminded herself. Still, it was hard not to worry.

"Have fun," she said instead. "We'll catch up at dinner?"

"Yeah, sure thing," Amelia replied over her shoulder, already rushing out the door again.

Charlotte sighed, turning back to the window. So much change, so fast. She could only pray they were headed for brighter shores. Charlotte watched Amelia hurry down the garden path and out the front gate, her daughter's carefree spirit both enviable and concerning. She knew Amelia was exploring her newfound independence, but Charlotte wished they could share more of this journey together.

Left alone again in the vastness of the ballroom, Charlotte's gaze returned to the restless sea. She reached for her phone, scrolling through her contacts until she found Roxanne's name. She hesitated for a moment, remembering the unreturned text from the day before. With a deep breath, she tapped out a new message:

"Roxanne, can we talk? I really need my sister right now."

She hit send, hoping for a response this time, but the immediate silence from her phone was disheartening. Charlotte set the device aside, feeling a twinge of loneliness.

Her thoughts then turned to Simon. She remembered his text from earlier, saying he'd be working late. With Isla in town, Charlotte couldn't help but feel a bit uneasy. She quickly composed a message to him:

"Hope work is going well. Just checking in. Miss you."

She knew he was probably too busy to reply right away, but sending the message gave her a small sense of connection. Her phone remained quiet, adding to the growing sense of isolation.

With a heavy heart, Charlotte turned her attention back to her painting. She picked up her brush, dipped it in paint, and tried to lose herself in the strokes. The canvas before her was a landscape of the cove, but her brushstrokes were hesitant, lacking the usual passion she poured into her art. Frustrated, Charlotte set down her brush, stepping back to look at her work. The painting was a reflection of her inner state: fragmented, unresolved, a mix of vibrant hues and somber shades. She realized she was trying to paint calmness into a scene that was as turbulent as her emotions.

With a sigh, Charlotte cleaned her brushes, her mind still a whirlpool of thoughts. She decided to give herself a break, hoping that a little distance might bring clarity to both her art and her life. She turned off the lights, leaving the ballroom and its unfinished painting behind, stepping out into the bright morning light, searching for a moment of peace amidst the chaos.

***

The moment's peace had not come until evening. After the ballroom, Charlotte had been kept so occupied by her guests that she hadn't been able to break free until late in the evening.

Now, Charlotte clicked off the bedside lamp, enveloping her room in darkness. She slid under the cool sheets, the soft mattress molding to her weary body. She closed her eyes, yearning for the oblivion of sleep, but her mind continued to churn.

Isla. The name drifted through Charlotte's thoughts like a haunting refrain. She pictured Isla's flawless features and stylish clothes, so effortlessly elegant. Charlotte glanced down at her faded pajamas, feeling frumpy and dull in comparison.

With a sigh, she rolled over, punching her pillow in frustration. She couldn't understand what brought Isla here after all these years. Did she want Simon back? The idea made Charlotte's stomach knot.

"Get it together," she muttered to herself. This wasn't high school. She refused to feel threatened by Isla's beauty or the complicated history she shared with Simon.

Still...questions gnawed at her. What happened between them? Why did Isla leave Simon so suddenly? And why return now?

Charlotte groaned, rubbing her temples. She couldn't make sense of it tonight. Right now, she needed rest. The old inn creaked around her as she burrowed deeper under the covers. Tomorrow she would face things with a clear head.

For now, she focused on relaxing her mind, listening to the distant surf. Gradually her breathing slowed and her limbs grew heavy. As she hovered at the edge of sleep, her last conscious thought was of Simon. She wished he were here now, holding her close as the shadows gathered.

Charlotte drifted into a deep sleep, her worries temporarily fading away. As she entered the realm of dreams, the scene around her began to transform.

She found herself wandering the halls of the inn, bathed in moonlight streaming through the windows. There was an eerie quality to the stillness, like the calm before a storm.

Suddenly, a bright light flashed before Charlotte's eyes. She raised her hand to shield her face as the glow intensified. When she lowered her arm, she gasped in astonishment.

There, hovering in the air, was Isla. But she looked nothing like her usual self. Isla's slender frame was now adorned with gossamer wings, her hair spilled over her shoulders in golden waves. She wore a dress made of flower petals, vines curling around her arms and legs.

Charlotte blinked hard, trying to dispel this vision. But the winged Isla remained, regarding her with an impish grin. Then, in a high, singsong voice, she cried, "Come catch me if you can!"

With that, Isla zipped down the hallway in a streak of light. Charlotte hurried after her, stunned and confused. What was happening? She had to be dreaming - there was no other explanation.

Isla flitted just ahead, always out of reach. She trailed glitter in her wake, leaving the floors slick. Charlotte slid along the hardwood in her socks, arms windmilling to keep her balance.

"Isla, wait!" she called out in exasperation. But Isla merely giggled and continued her aerial acrobatics.

Charlotte pursued doggedly, determined to catch this puzzling, pixie version of Isla. But the fairy was crafty, disappearing in bursts of light whenever Charlotte drew near.

Charlotte shook her head in weary bafflement. Would this bizarre dream never end? Charlotte chased Isla down the stairs, sliding precariously on the glittery floor. She grabbed the banister to keep from tumbling head over heels.

At the bottom, Isla hovered, waggling her fingers in a tiny wave. Then she blew a handful of glitter right at Charlotte's face. Sputtering, Charlotte swiped at the shimmering dust. When she could see again, Isla had vanished once more.

"That's it!" Charlotte yelled, stamping her foot. She was through with these games.

Just then, a noise came from the kitchen - the unmistakable clatter of pots and pans. Charlotte hurried toward it, intent on catching Isla red-handed.

She skidded to a stop in the doorway. There stood Isla amidst a whirlwind of cooking implements swirling through the air. Charlotte watched in astonishment as Isla conducted the symphony of clanging metal with a wooden spoon.

"Bravo!" Charlotte said, clapping slowly. "You've had your fun. Now come down from there."

Isla smirked and cried, "Never!" Then she zoomed up the chimney in a burst of soot.

Charlotte coughed, waving away the cloud of dust. Though frustrated, she had to admit - this dream Isla had style. With a wry chuckle, she set off again in pursuit of the elusive fairy. Charlotte hurried into the dining room, following the sound of clattering and clanking. She skidded to a stop in the doorway, mouth falling open at the bizarre scene before her.

There, in the middle of the grand room, was a troupe of dancing lobsters. Their bulky bodies swayed and shuffled in time to an upbeat melody. Their claws clicked together rhythmically as they twirled and pirouetted across the floor.

Isla stood atop the large dining table, conducting them with a baton. "Come on, my lovelies! Pick up the tempo!" she cried.

The lobsters moved faster, spinning and side-stepping with unexpected grace. Charlotte watched, dumbfounded. She had to admit, it was an impressive production.

"Bravo, bravo!" Isla cheered, as the lobsters finished with a flashy claw-clacking finale. "Encore, encore!"

The lobsters scuttled back into formation, ready to perform again. Charlotte stepped forward and cleared her throat loudly.

"Alright, that's quite enough!" she announced, hands on her hips. "Shoo! Out with you!"

She waved her arms at the creatures, trying to herd them toward the door. They clicked their claws in protest but obeyed, waddling out in a straight line.

Isla pouted. "You're no fun!" She vanished in a puff of glitter.

Charlotte sighed, surveying the lobster-littered room. "What a bizarre dream," she muttered, shaking her head. Despite the madness, she had to smile. Leave it to her subconscious to create such an eccentric diversion from her real-life worries.

Charlotte's amusement was short-lived. There was a loud whooshing sound from outside. She hurried to the window and looked up. Floating high above the inn was a massive, iridescent hot air balloon. The basket beneath it was empty, but Charlotte could see Isla's tiny form perched atop the balloon itself.

"Oh no," Charlotte groaned. What was Isla up to now?

The balloon drifted lazily over the buildings, casting an enormous, slowly moving shadow across the village. Windows and doors opened below as people stepped outside to investigate the strange sight. Pointing fingers and exclamations of shock rose up.

Isla stood tall, hands on her hips. "Attention, good people!" she cried, her high voice magically amplified. "May I present my latest whimsical creation!"

With a dramatic wave of her hand, the balloon began spewing glitter in all directions. It rained down on the streets and buildings like multicolored snow.

Charlotte watched in dismay as the village was quickly covered in a layer of sparkling glitter. It was harmless, but incredibly messy. This would take forever to clean up!

She scanned the chaotic scene, looking for a way to stop this glittery onslaught. Her eyes fell upon a box of push pins on a nearby desk. That might work! She grabbed a fistful of the pins and rushed back to the window just as the balloon drifted nearer.

Taking careful aim, Charlotte began launching pins at the floating behemoth. They bounced harmlessly off its rubbery surface. Isla cackled with delight.

"You'll have to try harder than that!" she taunted.

Charlotte gritted her teeth. This required a more strategic approach. The balloon swayed teasingly as it moved, making it a difficult target. She tracked its movement, timing the rhythm of its drift. Just as it paused, she let fly another pin. This one hit its mark, piercing the surface. There was a small pop, and glitter spewed from the new hole.

"Yes!" Charlotte cheered. One down, many more to go.

Charlotte repeated her strategic process, timing each throw carefully. One by one, more holes appeared in the massive balloon as her pins found their targets. Isla shrieked in protest as her glittery weapon began deflating rapidly.

"No! My beautiful balloon!"

Charlotte ignored her cries, focused intently on her task. With a final well-placed throw, the balloon gave a mighty groan as the largest hole yet opened up. Then, it erupted in a deafening BANG!

Glitter and balloon scraps rained down as Charlotte shielded her eyes. When she lowered her arm and surveyed the scene, the streets were covered in a layer of sparkling confetti. Villagers emerged from buildings to gawk at the bizarre sight.

And there, in the midst of it all, stood Isla with a scowl. The two women locked eyes for a tense moment before Isla vanished in her signature puff of smoke, leaving only echoes of her frustrated screams.

Charlotte jolted awake in bed, heart racing. She sat up, blinking in confusion as the intensity of the vivid dream lingered. Glancing around the quiet room, she slowly realized it had just been a dream.

"Well, that was...something," she muttered, shaking her head. A wry smile crossed her lips as the absurdity sunk in. Perhaps her subconscious was trying to send her a message about Isla. If so, it certainly had chosen a creative way to do it.

Charlotte glanced at the clock on her nightstand, the glowing numbers telling her it was nearly midnight. There was no sound from the rest of the house, making her suspect that Amelia hadn't returned home. A frown creased her brow.

Where could she be at this hour? Was she alright? Charlotte felt a knot of worry forming in her stomach. She knew Amelia had likely gone out with Nathan. Charlotte debated whether to call or text, not wanting to seem paranoid. But it was so late, and she hadn't checked in. As a mom, she couldn't shake the nagging concern.

Making a decision, she reached for her phone on the nightstand. Pulling up Amelia's number, she typed out a text:

Just checking in. It's getting late, and I realized I haven't heard from you. Is everything okay? Let me know when you're on your way back. Thanks!

Charlotte read over the message, hoping it struck the right balance of care without sounding accusatory. With a deep breath, she hit send, then set the phone back down.

She sank back against her pillow, staring up at the ceiling fan as it spun lazily. Now there was nothing to do but wait and hope they'd return soon, safe and sound. Charlotte closed her eyes, trying to calm her restless thoughts. Tomorrow would be a new day, a chance to start fresh. For now, she just had to believe everything would work out.

Charlotte tossed and turned, unable to quiet her mind. Thoughts of Amelia and Simon mingled with the absurd dream she'd had earlier.

As she drifted in that hazy space between waking and sleep, the images from the dream flashed through her mind. Isla as a mischievous fairy, the dancing lobsters, the giant balloon. It had all felt so real in the moment. Now, as she lay in bed, Charlotte had to smile at the sheer ridiculousness of it all. Her subconscious had spun quite the tale.

While the dream had been stressful, it was also comically over the top. Charlotte realized her anxiety about Isla had manifested in the form of chaotic, almost slapstick humor. As Charlotte reflected, she felt her body start to relax. Her breathing deepened and her limbs grew heavy. The worries of the day seemed less ominous through the lens of humor.

With the ghost of a smile still on her lips, Charlotte finally surrendered to sleep. The fan continued its quiet rhythm overhead as she drifted off, ready to face a new day.

The night wore on, the old inn settling into silence as Charlotte drifted into a deep sleep. For the first time in weeks, her mind and body found tranquility, the stress of recent events finally releasing its grip. Shadows danced across the walls as the moonlight filtered in through the curtains. Charlotte's breathing was slow and steady, her expression smooth in repose. The frenetic energy that had possessed her earlier was now gone.

Curled beneath the covers, Charlotte embraced the rare gift of undisturbed rest. No creaking floorboards or passing cars interrupted her slumber. The fan hummed its lullaby, ushering her into soothing darkness.

For these few precious hours, Charlotte's worries could not reach her. The chaos surrounding Isla, the rift with Amelia, the crumbling state of the inn - all of it faded away. There was only the quiet rhythm of her heartbeat and the rise and fall of her chest.

CHAPTER FOURTEEN

The laptop wobbled on the worn oak desk in Charlotte's makeshift office, where she sat poised before the screen. With a soft click, the screen came to life, and her fingers danced nimbly over the keyboard, initiating the video call software with practiced ease. Her gaze, a blend of concentration and artistic intuition, scrutinized the camera angle – a tilt here, a swivel there – until her image was perfectly framed within the bounds of the digital window.

"Let's see," Charlotte murmured to herself, tapping at the volume icon on the screen. The small test chime echoed crisply through the room, a satisfactory herald to their impending conversation. She adjusted the microphone setting, ensuring her voice would carry clearly across the ocean that lay between her and Roxanne.

"Come on, Roxie," she whispered as the seconds ticked by, her anticipation bubbling like a delicate champagne fizzing in her chest. The cursor blinked in the corner of the chat window, its rhythm a silent metronome to her rising eagerness.

Through the open window, a sea breeze teased the edge of her papers, carrying with it the scent of salt and the distant murmur of waves against the shore. The Old Crown Inn, with its crumbling walls and whispers of yesteryears, seemed to hold its breath alongside Charlotte as she waited in the midday hush.

Her thoughts began to drift, unfurling like the tendrils of ivy that clung to the inn's façade. *Isla.* The name brought an involuntary tightening to Charlotte's features – a mixture of wariness and a hope she couldn't quite smother. Could Isla truly be seeking closure, or was this some ploy, a shadow from Simon's past reaching out to disrupt the fragile peace they'd begun to build?

"Darn it," Charlotte sighed, pressing a hand to her forehead. The questions multiplied, each one a tiny incision in the fabric of her trust. If only Roxanne could help her untangle the knot of uncertainties that tightened with every thought of Isla.

A soft ping snapped Charlotte back to the present, and she looked up to see Roxanne's familiar username pop into the 'waiting room' of the call. A smile touched Charlotte's lips, but it was a soldier's smile – ready, resolute, and tinged with the gravity of the upcoming discourse.

"Connecting..." The word flashed on the screen, a digital drumroll to the moment she'd been waiting for, and suddenly Roxanne's face appeared, vibrant and reassuring as always.

"Charlotte! There's my intrepid sister," Roxanne exclaimed, her sassy tone a welcome melody that swept through the static distance.

"Roxie, I'm so glad you're here," Charlotte replied, the relief in her voice mingling with the undertow of worry. "There's something I need to talk to you about – it's about Simon." Her fingers fidgeted with the hem of her blouse, a telltale sign of the nervous energy that pulsed beneath her calm exterior.

"Spill it, Char. You know I've got your back," Roxanne said, her eyes sharp but kind, the bond of sisterhood a beacon in the fog of Charlotte's unease. "And I'm sorry about the text—work has been so crazy this week."

The sun dipped lower outside the window, painting the room in hues of fading orange and pink, as if the sky itself lent its ear to the confidences about to be shared. And there, amid the echoes of a life she'd left behind in New York and the rugged beauty of Chesham Cove that whispered promises of healing, Charlotte readied herself to bare her soul.

Charlotte's gaze was locked onto Roxanne's image on the screen, the glow from her laptop casting a spectral sheen across the canvas of worry etched upon her face. "Roxie," she began, her voice quivering like a violin string pulled too taut, "I know you got the text, but there's more. I want to believe that this woman, Isla, who's staying at The Crown is just looking for closure with Simon. That this surprise visit isn't going to stir up old ghosts."

"Charlotte, darling," Roxanne's voice was firm, unwavering, "Most ex-wives are not the sort to look back, much less seek closure. They are always playing chess, thinking three moves ahead."

Charlotte's heart did a slow, torturous somersault. Her fingers stilled, the hem of her blouse now lying forgotten in her lap. How could she reconcile the desire to see the good in someone with the stark reality painted by Roxanne's words?

Roxanne leaned closer to the camera, her eyes reflecting a history of protective instincts. "You can't let your guard down, Char. Not around her."

A sigh escaped Charlotte, trailing into the quietude of the room. The Old Crown Inn seemed to hold its breath alongside her, the walls steeped in stories of bygone days and echoes of whispers that might well have been her own doubts crawling along the aged woodwork.

"Part of me wonders if I'm just being paranoid..." Charlotte murmured, more to herself than to Roxanne. She wrapped her arms around her torso as if to steady the fluttering uncertainty within. "If maybe—just maybe—she really has moved on."

"Paranoid? Charlotte, you're the most level-headed person I know." Roxanne's lips thinned, a line drawn in sisterly solidarity.

"True," Charlotte conceded, her eyes drifting to the view out the window. It was a painter's dream, but today it only mirrored the muddled palette of her thoughts.

Her mind teemed with the memories of conversations past, laughter shared over wine glasses, promises made under starry skies—all with Simon. Could Isla's return shatter the delicate peace she'd built in this quaint coastal refuge?

Okay, Charlotte," Roxanne's voice finally broke through the speakers, "you need to be smart about this. Isla's a fox, sly and unpredictable. Start by gathering some intel, nonchalantly. You live in a small town now; use that to your advantage."

"Intel?" Charlotte echoed, her brow furrowed as she considered Roxanne's suggestion. Her fingers ceased their tapping, instead now tracing the grain of the wood beneath them. "You mean like... asking around?"

"Exactly!" Roxanne's face lit up with enthusiasm. "People talk, Charlotte. There's bound to be someone who's seen her, knows her routine. And you've got that charming innkeeper persona – play it up."

A hesitant smile tugged at the corners of Charlotte's lips. She could picture herself, a detective in her own drama, casually inquiring about Isla under the guise of polite conversation over breakfast scones. "I suppose I do have a knack for making people feel comfortable enough to spill their secrets," she mused aloud.

"See? You're a natural." Roxanne leaned forward, her eyes earnest. "Just remember, whatever you find out, communication with Simon is key. Secrets between you two will only give Isla an edge if she's plotting something."

The mention of Simon sent a warm flutter through Charlotte's chest, a stark contrast to the icy knot of uncertainty that had taken residence there. She was conflicted—and she wondered if she could trust him. She wanted to, but...

"I know," she admitted, her voice barely above a whisper. "I don't want any barriers between us. Trust is the foundation we're building on. But that's not all up to me."

"Good. Don't shoulder all of this yourself. He should be trying to keep that communication line open, no matter what."

Charlotte nodded, absorbing Roxanne's words as they resonated within her. She felt a burgeoning sense of gratitude for her sister's unwavering support, for the guidance that seemed to light a path through the fog of anxiety. "Thank you, Roxy. I don't know what I'd do without you."

"Ah, you'd manage," Roxanne said with a dismissive wave, though her smile was affectionate. "But you never have to. I'm here."

The sisters shared a moment of understanding, a silent acknowledgment of the unspoken pact that bound them.

"Deep down," Charlotte confessed, her voice barely above a whisper, "the thought of confronting her makes my bones cold. But I can't shake the feeling that there's something more behind her sudden reappearance."

"Then trust that instinct," Roxanne encouraged, her tone softened, a blend of empathy and resolve. "You've always had a keen sense, especially when it comes to people. If your gut says there's more, then there likely is."

"Thank you, Roxie. Sometimes I just need to hear it from you to believe it myself," Charlotte admitted, allowing a small smile to surface amidst the sea of her concerns. Her sister's conviction was a lighthouse guiding her through the stormy doubt that clouded her mind.

"Always," Roxanne affirmed, her presence a steadfast anchor. "Now, what's your plan?"

Charlotte drew in a deep breath, exhaled slowly, and squared her shoulders. With Roxanne's support fortifying her resolve, she prepared to navigate the treacherous waters ahead. She would confront Isla. She would protect the life she was building with Simon. And come what may, she would do it with the strength that had carried her across an ocean to a new beginning in Chesham Cove.

Charlotte's fingers trembled slightly as she brushed a lock of chestnut hair behind her ear, the screen before her flickering with the weak call signal. The Old Crown Inn's study, usually a sanctuary of solace for her art, now felt like the stage for an uncertain drama. The walls lined with bookshelves and the scent of salt air drifting through the open window did little to calm her.

The call wound down with promises of future support, and Charlotte sat back in her chair, her gaze lingering on the now blank screen. The inn around her was quiet, save for the occasional creak of aged wood—a testament to the resilience of things that stand the test of time.

"Simon," she murmured, allowing his name to anchor her thoughts. With each repetition, her resolve crystallized, and she knew what she must do. Confrontation was never easy, but neither was the path that had led her to this rugged English coast, to the man who had reignited the embers of her once-dimmed spirit.

"Alright, I'll start my... investigation tomorrow," Charlotte declared, her voice laced with a newfound determination.

"Good. Just keep me posted, okay? And Charlotte," Roxanne added, her tone softening, "be careful. We both know how cunning an ex can be."

"I will be," Charlotte promised, feeling the weight of the task ahead. Yet, despite the gravity, there was a steely resolve in her posture, a quiet strength that came from knowing she was not alone in her quest. The thought sent a shiver down her spine, not of fear, but of the chilling realization of how much was at stake. Her relationship with Simon, the tranquility of her newfound home, the harmony she yearned for Amelia—everything hinged on unearthing Isla's true intentions.

She hung up and let her gaze drift to the cold remnants of tea in her cup, the once-steaming liquid now a pool reflecting her troubled thoughts. The chipped rim, a flaw she'd come to cherish, reminded her that imperfection could tell the most compelling stories. She stood up, pushing the chair back with a quiet scrape against the wooden floor, and moved toward the fireplace.

"Tomorrow, I face her. Tomorrow, I learn the truth." Charlotte ran her fingers along the mantelpiece, tracing the intricate carvings that had witnessed countless confessions and heart-to-hearts over generations. It was time to add her own story to its legacy. With that, Charlotte stepped out of the room, leaving behind the echoes of her declaration.

CHAPTER FIFTEEN

The morning air held a crispness that was unexpected. Charlotte Moore, with her artist's eye for detail, couldn't help but admire the way the early light danced on the cobblestones of Chesham Cove as she set out from The Old Crown Inn. She had been in England long enough now to appreciate the subtle shifts of the seasons and find solace in the enduring beauty of the harbor town.

She wore a loose-fitting cardigan over her blouse, blending effortlessly into the morning bustle. Her gaze followed Isla Wagner, whose elegant silhouette moved with purpose through the awakening streets. Isla's heels clicked rhythmically against the stones—a metronome to Charlotte's cautious steps.

"Where are you off to this fine morning?" Charlotte murmured to herself, keeping her voice low and drowned out by the chatter around her. There was something about Isla, an enigma wrapped in the guise of Simon's soon-to-be-ex-wife, that piqued Charlotte's curiosity.

Isla's shoulders were pulled back, her posture almost defiant as she navigated the narrow lanes leading toward the harbor. Charlotte noted the nervous energy in Isla's occasional glance backward, the sweep of her eyes betraying a vigilance that seemed out of place on such a serene day.

"Looking for someone? Or hoping not to be found?" Charlotte pondered, her thoughts trailing Isla like an invisible tether. She kept her distance, just another face among the townspeople starting their day.

"Excuse me, dear," an elderly woman said as she bumped into Charlotte, who had momentarily slowed to keep her surveillance discreet.

"Sorry," Charlotte replied with a soft smile, stepping aside. She could not afford to attract attention lest Isla notice her presence.

As they neared the harbor, the scent of salt and seaweed grew stronger. The cries of seagulls overhead mingled with the creaks of boats swaying gently in their moorings. Isla's pace didn't waver; her eyes were now fixed on the horizon, scanning the masts and sails as if seeking a particular vessel or perhaps its captain.

"Always the artist, always observing," Charlotte mused inwardly, trying to decipher the story behind Isla's searching gaze. "But what story am I part of here? What picture am I painting merely by following her?"

Charlotte felt a twinge of guilt for her surreptitious behavior, yet the mystery of Isla's intentions held her captive. It was as though she had stumbled upon a hidden piece of her new life that demanded to be brought into the light. Perhaps it was this cove, with its layers of history and secrets, that whispered to her soul—an echo of the new beginnings she sought.

"Could it be Simon she's looking for?" Charlotte allowed the thought to linger, even as she questioned her own motivations. Was it concern for her daughter, Amelia, caught up in this tangled web of relationships, or a deeper, more personal need to unravel the threads of past loves and losses?

The brisk walk and the chill in the air had flushed Charlotte's cheeks by the time they approached the waterfront. Isla's figure, now outlined against the backdrop of bobbing boats, remained unaware of the watchful eyes tracing her every move.

"Whatever truths you're hiding, Isla Wagner," Charlotte whispered under her breath, her artist's intuition bristling, "I intend to find them."

The quaint shops of Chesham Cove, each with their own tales etched in weathered signs and salt-worn facades, seemed to huddle together as if bracing against the encroaching modernity that Thomas Windnell threatened to bring. Charlotte moved among them like a shadow, her eyes never leaving the slender figure of Isla Wagner who drifted ahead, an enigma wrapped in an elegant overcoat.

"Keep it casual, Charlotte," she murmured to herself, tucking a loose strand of hair behind her ear as she sidestepped into an alcove to let a group of chattering tourists pass by. Studying the posters of local events plastered on the wall beside her, she pretended to be engrossed in the details of an upcoming art exhibition.

"Charming place you've chosen to settle in," a voice observed from amongst the crowd. Charlotte glanced up, offering a noncommittal smile to the kind-faced woman who had noticed her lingering.

"Isn't it?" Charlotte replied, her gaze stealing back to Isla, who was now slowing her pace. "Every corner seems to hold a story."

"Or a secret," the woman added with a knowing nod before being swept away by her companions.

Charlotte felt a shiver trace her spine—not from the cool sea air, but from the truth hidden in those words. She pressed on, her boots clicking softly against the cobblestones, careful to maintain the delicate distance between herself and Isla.

The harbor's presence grew stronger with each step, the scent of brine intertwining with the aroma of fresh-baked bread from the nearby bakery. The sound of seagulls quarreling over scraps provided a natural soundtrack to the coastal ballet of residents and visitors alike.

And then, Isla came to an abrupt halt.

Through the throng of people, Charlotte glimpsed the display window that had captured Isla's attention—a jewelry store, its wares glinting seductively under the soft glow of tastefully arranged spotlights. Pearls lay nestled in velvet, gold chains looped in lazy elegance, and silver charms winked at potential admirers.

"What is it that fascinates you so, Isla?" she wondered, her artist's eye analyzing the display, searching for a clue in the array of precious artifacts.

Isla's profile was etched with concentration, her lips parted slightly as though about to speak to the treasures beyond the glass. Her hand lifted, hovering just inches from the window before falling back to her side, a gesture filled with longing—or was it regret?

"Are you shopping for a memory or trying to forget one?" Charlotte pondered, the question hanging silently between them.

She wanted to reach out, to ask Isla directly, to understand the silent story unfolding before her. But the chasm of their unspoken history and Charlotte's role as the outsider—the intruder in this intimate moment—held her back.

"Patience," Charlotte told herself, her heart heavy with the complexities of human connections. "Every piece will fall into place in time." And with that thought anchoring her, she watched and waited, the observer once more, as the dance of understanding between two souls played on in silence.

Charlotte edged closer to the neighboring shop, a quaint antiquarian bookstore whose window boasted an array of leather-bound classics and first editions. She positioned herself so that her reflection appeared to be absorbed by the titles on display, while her gaze remained covertly fixed on Isla through the bookstore's ornate, gold-leafed mirror propped against the wall.

"Isn't it a treasure trove?" murmured Charlotte, admiring the window. "Every book is a doorway to another world." Her fingers traced the spine of an old novel as if considering it, but her attention was elsewhere. Through the artifice of her reflection, she watched Isla stare intently at the jewelry store across the cobbled street.

The afternoon light dappling through the leaves of nearby trees cast a mosaic of shadows and warm sunspots on the pavement. Charlotte noted how the shifting patterns seemed to reflect Isla's indecision, the play of uncertainty across her features.

"Are you looking for a gift or something more... personal, Isla?" Charlotte pondered internally, the question forming like a delicate sketch in her mind. It was a curious thing, watching someone when they believed themselves to be alone with their thoughts—like spying a solitary figure through the mist, details obscured, intentions veiled.

She observed Isla tilt her head, her hair cascading over one shoulder—a waterfall of secrets. Isla's eyes darted from the jewelry to the throng of people passing by, searching for a face among the crowd. Was she expecting someone? Fearful of being recognized?

"Something's amiss," Charlotte thought, the suspicion coiling tighter within her chest. "But what?"

Her own breath fogged the glass briefly as she feigned interest in the antiquities around her. She picked up a small, carved wooden box, admiring its craftsmanship, all the while keeping one eye on the scene unfolding outside.

"Is he here yet?" Charlotte imagined Isla whispering to herself, though no words escaped Isla's lips. The ex-wife's body language spoke volumes—her stance rigid yet poised to flee, her hands clasping and unclasping at her sides.

"Who are you waiting for, Isla? And why does it feel like you're holding your breath?"

A pang of empathy struck Charlotte, remembering times she too had been caught in a web of anticipation and dread. But this was not her story; she was merely a spectator, trying to decipher the plot from scattered pages.

"Patience," she reminded herself once more, placing the wooden box back on its shelf with a soft click. "All will be revealed when the time is right."

With a sigh, Charlotte continued her ruse, her heart a canvas of curiosity and concern, painting every glance and gesture of the woman outside in strokes of muted wonder and shaded doubt.

The harbor's chill breeze toyed with the loose strands of Charlotte's hair, carrying the scent of brine and old wood. She shifted from foot to foot, her gaze anchored on Isla who still lingered by the jewelry store window. The cobblestone streets of Chesham Cove echoed with the chatter of passersby, but the murmurs seemed distant, filtered through the lens of Charlotte's focused observation.

Caught in the act of surveillance, she held her breath as the unmistakable figure of Amelia approached. The young girl moved with a carefree stride, her laughter mingling with the seagulls' cries overhead, her college youth shining like a beacon amidst the sea-worn faces of the town.

"Amelia here? Now?" Charlotte's thoughts spun, a whirlpool of concern muddying her previously clear intentions. "She mustn't see me like this—"

But fate had already cast its die. Amelia's eyes, the same hazel that had once looked up at Charlotte with unwavering trust, now narrowed in suspicion as they landed on the hidden tableau before her. There was her mother, seemingly skulking behind a display window, and not far off, Isla, the woman whose enigma had drawn Charlotte into this silent dance of shadows and secrets.

"Mom?" Amelia's voice sliced through the coastal symphony, sharp and disbelieving. "What are you doing here?"

Charlotte turned, her heart fluttering against her ribs like a caged bird. "Oh, darling, I was just—" She hesitated, the truth too convoluted to explain, too fragile to hold against the weight of her daughter's confusion.

"Are you following me?" Amelia's accusation hung between them, a storm cloud threatening to burst. "Because I'm dating Nathan, isn't it?"

"Amelia, no, it's not like that," Charlotte began, her hands reaching out only to fall back to her sides, the gesture as incomplete as her explanation.

"Then what is it?" Amelia demanded, her stance rigid, her expression a tangled masterpiece of hurt and defiance.

"Sweetheart, I can assure you, my being here has nothing to do with you or Nathan." Charlotte's voice was soft, a brushstroke attempting to smooth over the jagged edges of misunderstanding. "I mean, I saw you both the other night, at the Wavem but—"

"Right." Amelia's laugh was hollow, an echo chamber reflecting back Charlotte's own fears of losing her daughter's faith. "I should've known better than to believe you'd just let me live my life."

"Amelia..." Charlotte's plea trailed off as Amelia turned away, her shoulders set against the backdrop of quaint shops and bobbing boats. "Please, love, listen to me," Charlotte whispered, a plea lost to the wind, watching Amelia merge with the crowd until she became another part of the scenery, leaving Charlotte adrift in the wake of their fractured encounter.

"Patience," she coaxed herself, though the word tasted like ash in her mouth. Giving Amelia space felt akin to placing a bandage on a wound that required stitches—necessary, but insufficient. Steeling herself against the surge of regret, Charlotte turned her attention back to Isla. There was more at play here than personal grievances; there was a puzzle needing to be solved. It seemed Isla, too, had noticed Amelia's abrupt departure, for her posture had stiffened, the tension in her frame apparent even from a distance.

"Who could warrant such vigilance?" Charlotte wondered, her artistic eye capturing the nuances of Isla's behavior, the silent narrative unfolding before her.

"Whatever secret you're keeping, Isla Wagner, it leads to the harbor," Charlotte resolved, her spirit reigniting with purpose. And yet, beneath her determination lay an undercurrent of sorrow, the realization that her pursuit of one truth had momentarily cost her another.

The sun dappled the cobblestones of Chesham Cove's main thoroughfare, casting a myriad of shifting patterns that seemed to mock Charlotte's clandestine pursuit. She tucked herself behind an ancient brick wall adorned with creeping ivy, her gaze firmly fixed on Isla's back as she lingered near the jewelry store.

With the taste of remorse heavy on her tongue, Charlotte shifted her gaze back toward Isla, who remained fixated on the jewelry store's window, oblivious to the storm of emotions swirling just yards away.

The air wrapped around Charlotte, thick with the scent of salt and sorrow. She took a deep breath, inhaling the briny resolve of the sea, allowing it to fill her lungs, to steel her spine.

Amidst the distant call of gulls and the murmur of passersby, Charlotte reaffirmed her commitment to the truth. She had to know why Isla was here, what secret danced behind those contemplative eyes. And perhaps in unearthing Isla's mystery, she might find the key to mending the fractured bond with her own flesh and blood.

"Patience," she reminded herself once more, though the word felt like a pebble in her shoe, uncomfortable and persistent. "In time, all will be revealed."

Charlotte's eyes lingered on the diminishing silhouette of Amelia, her heart caught in a vice of maternal concern and self-reproach. The colorful array of tourists bobbing through the streets seemed to absorb her daughter's form, rendering her a vanishing point amidst the tapestry of Chesham Cove's midday bustle.

"Amelia," Charlotte whispered, the name barely escaping her lips before it was snatched away by the coastal wind. Her fingers twitched with the urge to reach out, to pull her daughter back from the tide of misunderstanding that swept between them.

She watched as Amelia paused momentarily at the street corner, her posture rigid like the masts of the docked ships, then turned sharply, disappearing from view. Charlotte's heart pounded against her ribs, keeping time with the rhythmic sloshing of the harbor waters against the quay.

Resigned, Charlotte turned back to the task at hand, her gaze flitting back to Isla's stationary figure. An inexplicable sense of duty anchored her to this moment, to the unraveling enigma that was Isla's presence here, by the jewelry store and the restless sea beyond.

Charlotte's fingers trailed over the coarse fabric of the fisherman's jackets hanging on a peg outside the chandlery, her touch as absent as her gaze. Her mind was a whirlpool of thoughts, eddying around the recent scene with Amelia – each replay adding a fresh layer of frustration and regret. Yet, like a painter who must step back to see the whole canvas, she refocused her attention on the woman who had initiated this entire charade - Isla.

"Excuse me," she murmured to a passerby as she edged closer to the harbor front, brushing past clusters of tourists and locals alike. The scent of salt and seaweed wrapped around her, a familiar embrace that usually brought comfort. But not today.

"Is she meeting someone?" Charlotte pondered silently, observing Isla's body language. The tilt of her head, the way her eyes darted, searching, expectant. "Or is it something—or someone—she's waiting for?"

Isla's heels clacked against the cobblestones, a steady rhythm that Charlotte matched with quieter steps. She watched Isla pause again, pretending to admire a cluster of boats bobbing in the water, their colorful hulls a stark contrast against the gray-blue of the chilly English Channel.

"Beautiful, isn't it?" a voice broke through her concentration, a local fisherman acknowledging the view with a nod toward the boats.

"Truly," Charlotte replied, her gaze never leaving Isla. "Though sometimes, what lies beneath the surface is even more intriguing."

"Isn't that the truth," the fisherman chuckled before moving on, oblivious to the subtext woven into their brief exchange.

Charlotte's artist's eye caught the subtle play of light reflecting off the water, casting prismatic colors onto Isla's entranced face. "What are you looking at?" she whispered under her breath, inching forward to gain a better vantage point.

The answer came as a jolt, sending a cold ripple down her spine. There, emerging from a side street that led directly to the docks, was Simon. Rugged, his coat flapping in the wind, he carried the unmistakable aura of a man who belonged to the sea.

"Simon..." The name escaped her lips, a silent exclamation. A revelation crystallized in her mind; the puzzle pieces slotted together with stunning clarity. "She's stalking Simon."

Charlotte felt her pulse quicken, her hands clenched into fists as she ducked behind a stack of lobster traps. From this new angle, she could see the intensity in Isla's eyes—a fierce, almost predatory focus. It was clear that whatever unresolved history they shared, it still had a powerful hold on Isla.

"Darn it, Isla, what game are you playing?"

CHAPTER SIXTEEN

The Old Crown Inn seemed to groan in the whispering wind as Charlotte pushed through its heavy, oak door. Sunlight filtered through stained glass windows, casting kaleidoscopic patterns that danced mockingly on the faded wallpaper. Charlotte's chest heaved with fatigue and her gaze swept across the quiet lobby, past the grand staircase with its worn carpet runner, and then it halted. There, leaning casually against the reception desk, was a figure that made Charlotte's heart sink further into the pit of her stomach.

Isla Wagner stood draped in effortless elegance, her willowy frame clad in something chic yet simple, a stark contrast to the antiquated charm of the inn. Her presence was like a drop of ink in clear water, spreading and impossible to ignore. Next to her was Thomas Windnell.

"Charlotte," Isla called out, her voice smooth as poured cream, but with a hint of frost that could chill the bones. "I didn't expect to see you back so soon."

"Nor did I expect to find you here, Isla," Charlotte responded, the muscles in her jaw flexing as she struggled to maintain cordiality. Charlotte had expected to be able to dash out and come back before anyone else was stirring at The Crown—but that was obviously not possible. She could feel the weight of Isla's cool appraisal, the silent judgment that seemed to question every choice Charlotte had made since arriving in Chesham Cove. "Or you, Thomas."

"Oh, we just met here, waiting for you," Thomas explained. "May I have a word?"

"You may not," Charlotte said, savoring the shock on their faces. "Excuse me," she said, brushing past Isla with a rigidity in her posture that defied the fatigue that clung to her limbs like ivy. She needed to regroup, to shake off the shadow that Thomas Windnell—and now Isla—cast over her sanctuary.

As she ascended the staircase, each step creaked underfoot, echoing her internal pledge. This inn, with its peeling paint and creaky floorboards, was her battlefield and her refuge, her canvas and her muse. She would not be swayed by slick city men or enigmatic ex-wives. The Old Crown Inn was hers, and every fiber of her being screamed that she would fight for it.

Charlotte's heels clacked against the wooden floorboards as she descended the staircase, her descent seemingly in rhythm with the hammering of her heart. The Old Crown Inn, with its labyrinthine corridors and rooms that whispered secrets of bygone eras, wrapped around her like a protective shawl. But the security it offered felt momentarily pierced as Thomas Windnell's silhouette loomed like an ominous cloud at the foot of the stairs.

"Charlotte, may I have a moment?" His voice was smooth, the words perfectly enunciated, each syllable a calculated step closer to his goal.

She paused on the final step, gripping the banister as if it were the mast of a ship caught in a storm. "Thomas," she acknowledged over the railing, not a quiver betraying the tempest brewing within.

"Your dedication to this place is admirable," he began, gesturing broadly to encompass the inn's rustic charm. "But you must consider the financial advantage of my offer."

"Offer? Advantage for whom?" Charlotte replied, each word laced with skepticism. It wasn't just money he was offering—it was surrender, capitulation to a future she didn't want.

Thomas jogged up the stairs, hand out. Charlotte's hand was trembling slightly as she took the folded paper from Thomas Windnell. She could feel the weight of his gaze, heavy with expectation, as she unfolded it with care not to tear the crisp edges. The numbers inside were neatly typed, each zero a round hole into a future she had never envisioned. Her heart thrummed in her chest at the sight—double the price of what she'd paid for The Old Crown Inn.

"Think of it, Charlotte," Thomas coaxed, his voice smooth like the fine silk of his tie. "That's financial freedom. Security for you and Amelia."

She let her eyes drift over the figures again, each digit a siren call to a life devoid of the worries that shadowed her dreams. Could money carve out a sanctuary from the relentless tides of change? The amount was staggering, a sum that could indeed secure a comfortable future, free of the chaos that had become her daily bread since moving to Chesham Cove.

But somewhere beneath the allure, something tightened in her chest—a visceral tug of war between the promise of wealth and the pull of her soul toward the inn's charming decay. The Old Crown Inn wasn't just mortar and stone to her; it was a canvas, weathered and worn, waiting for her to bring it back to life with careful strokes of love and perseverance.

"Why do you want this place so badly?" she questioned, narrowing her eyes at him.

"I have an interest in maintaining the local history, of course. My guests will want to come into town, see the sights. Maybe The Crown could become a second pub. Who knows?"

She sensed he was lying, but said nothing.

"Your daughter could go to any college," Thomas pressed on, mistaking her silence for consideration. "And think about it, no more scraping paint or dealing with leaky roofs."

Her fingers brushed against the paper as if it were a talisman capable of dispelling the storm of thoughts within her. For a fleeting moment, she saw herself elsewhere, unburdened by the ceaseless demands of renovation. A different life flickered before her eyes—one lined with ease instead of bristles dipped in paint.

Yet, as she held the offer in her hands, Charlotte's gaze unconsciously swept across the room, catching the slant of light as it danced upon the oak-paneled walls, the way it played hide and seek with the shadows, promising a day full of potential. Her breath caught in her throat. This inn, with its stubborn leaks and peeling wallpaper, was her testament to hope, a symbol of everything she had dared to dream since stepping away from the life she once knew.

"Money isn't the only currency I value, Thomas," she said at last, her voice steadier than she felt. The inn whispered through her, the gentle creaks and sighs of its old bones speaking of resilience and reinvention. It was more than an investment; it was a piece of her, intertwined with the wild beauty of the land and the community she was becoming a part of.

"Consider it," he urged one last time, the finality in his tone suggesting this was his end game.

"Thank you, but my decision stands," Charlotte replied, her conviction resonating deeper than the hollow echo of profit. The inn was more than a business venture—it was where her heart had chosen to anchor itself, amidst the rolling greenery and the salt-kissed air of Chesham Cove. It was home, and no amount of money could sever the roots she was nurturing here.

Charlotte's fingers trembled slightly as they enfolded the paper, its edges as sharp as the decision before her. Her gaze drifted upward, catching a glimpse of the wooden beams that stretched across the ceiling of The Old Crown Inn like the embrace of an old friend. She inhaled deeply, the scent of beeswax polish and aged wood filling her senses, grounding her. This was more than a building; it was a sanctuary she had resurrected with tender strokes of her artist's brush, infusing life into its every corner.

"Are you sure?" Thomas's voice broke through her reverie, his tone a mix of incredulity and something akin to admiration.

In her mind's eye, Charlotte saw the faces of the locals who had welcomed her, an outsider, with open arms. She thought of Amelia, her daughter, whose laughter echoed in these halls, chasing away the shadows of doubt. Yes, she was sure.

"Absolutely," she affirmed, her voice carrying the weight of her resolve. "This inn is my canvas, my community. It's where I've found a piece of myself I didn't know was lost."

Thomas watched her closely, his eyes searching for signs of faltering. But there was none to be found in the unwavering set of her jaw or the spark of passion that lit her eyes. Charlotte allowed herself a moment more of internal struggle, acknowledging the allure of financial ease, the promise of a future unburdened by the constant repairs and endless to-do lists. But then she thought of the laughter that filled the dining hall during evenings, the way the sun dipped below the horizon, painting the sea with strokes of gold and crimson, just beyond the inn's windows.

With a decisive motion, Charlotte's hand closed into a fist, crushing the paper along with the tempting offer it represented. The crinkle of the parchment was a symphony of rejection, each crease a note in her anthem of defiance.

"Then this is where our negotiation ends," Thomas concluded, the finality in his tone a stark contrast to the burgeoning sense of freedom swelling within Charlotte's chest.

"Indeed, it does," she replied, her eyes never leaving his. With one last look at the envelope, she shook her head. "This inn is more than just stone and timber, Mr. Windnell. It's hope. It's a new beginning. And I will not trade that for any sum."

Thomas's eyes narrowed ever so slightly, the corner of his mouth twitching in what could be annoyance or admiration—perhaps both. "You're making a mistake," he warned.

"Perhaps," she conceded, lifting her chin defiantly. "But it's my mistake to make. Now leave."

His presence seemed to fill the space, pressing in with the weight of his ambition, but Charlotte stood firm. She watched as he backed away, his departure no less imposing than his arrival. But as she turned, her hand brushed against the aged wood of the chair rail on the wall, feeling the etched grooves and imperfections beneath her fingertips—a tactile reminder of the inn's enduring strength and her own.

Isla was absent, having ghosted out as soon as the debate with Thomas had started. In the quiet that followed, Charlotte allowed herself a breath, deep and steadying. Her gaze wandered to the window where the English countryside lay spread out like a verdant tapestry, undulating hills and wildflowers swaying in the gentle breeze. This inn, this land—it was worth every ounce of struggle, every moment of doubt.

As she retreated to the sanctuary of her private quarters, she reminded herself why she had chosen this path. The inn was a living painting, one she intended to restore brushstroke by brushstroke. And she would do so not for profit, but for passion, for the preservation of beauty and history intertwined.

"Let him double his offers," she whispered to the empty room, her resolve a silent vow to the stones and beams that cradled her dreams. "The Old Crown Inn isn't just mine; it belongs to the story we're all still writing."

As Thomas retreated, Charlotte felt a profound connection to the inn tighten around her heart. It was a bond forged not in the currency of the realm but in the resilience of the human spirit. She turned away, her steps echoing softly on the stone floor, each one a testament to her journey—a path paved not with gold but with the rich tapestry of a life reborn among the rolling hills and whispering tides of Chesham Cove.

"Confound this wretched paint," she muttered, trying again to smooth the uneven coat on the window frame. The brush seemed to rebel in her hand, bristles splaying rebelliously, a splatter of eggshell white marking the glass like an unsolicited signature.

Her breath hitched, caught between exasperation and exhaustion. These walls, they absorbed more than just color; they soaked up her tension, her hope, her silent pleas for a fresh start. This inn was her canvas, but unlike the forgiving nature of paper, its textures fought back, challenging her with every stroke.

"Looks like you could use a hand... or perhaps a new brush," came a voice, tinged with an accent that curled around the edges like smoke.

Charlotte turned sharply, her movement dislodging another tool from the table—a hammer clattered to the ground, a punctuation mark on her surprise. Isla stood there, leaning casually against the doorway, arms crossed, golden hair cascading over her shoulders, eyes gleaming with a light that held both intrigue and mirth.

"Your technique could use some refinement," Isla said, the corners of her mouth twitching. "Though I suppose there's a certain... rustic charm to your approach."

"Rustic charm is exactly what I'm aiming for," Charlotte replied, hoping her tone conveyed more confidence than she felt at that moment.

"Ah, but charm doesn't patch up cracks or straighten crooked frames," Isla observed, moving closer to inspect the work. Charlotte noticed the delicate way Isla's fingers traced the edge of the windowsill, as if she could read its history with a touch.

"Sometimes," she began, her voice softening despite herself, "the imperfections are what make something truly beautiful." Her thoughts drifted to Daniel, to Amelia. How their own imperfections had once knitted together in a perfect tapestry of love and family, now frayed and unraveled.

"Perhaps. But imperfections don't pay the bills, nor do they shield you from the storms," Isla retorted, her gaze shifting to the clouds gathering outside, a portent of rain.

"Neither does standing around watching someone else work," Charlotte snapped back, regretting her tone almost instantly. It wasn't Isla's fault that Thomas Windnell's offer still fluttered temptingly in her mind, or that the inn demanded more from her than she'd anticipated.

"Touché." Isla's lips curved into a full smile now. "But tell me, Charlotte Moore of New York, did you come all this way to fight with wallpaper and wrestle with paint, or did you come here seeking something else?"

Charlotte let out a long sigh, her shoulders sagging slightly under the weight of unspoken truths. Seeking something else? Yes, she supposed she had been. A reprieve, a healing balm for the wounds left by a marriage dissolving like sugar in hot tea. She didn't answer, instead focusing on the unforgiving window frame, willing her hands to be steady.

"Maybe I did," she conceded after a moment, dipping the brush into the paint once more. "But right now, this inn is my battlefield. And I intend to win."

"Spoken like a true warrior," Isla said, a playful spark in her eye. "Just remember, even warriors need allies."

With that cryptic advice, Isla stepped back, allowing Charlotte the space to ponder her words. Allies, Charlotte thought. In the form of an enigmatic woman whose presence stirred as much curiosity as irritation? Maybe. Or perhaps in the form of the very walls that challenged her, teaching her resilience with every splinter and smear.

"New beginnings," she whispered, resuming her work with renewed vigor. "Healing." The mantra filled the room, intertwining with the scent of fresh paint and the creak of old timber. She worked not just to restore the inn's beauty but to carve out a sanctuary for her tattered spirit amidst the wild allure of Chesham Cove.

Charlotte's arm ached as she brandished the paintbrush like a sword, each stroke an attempt to reclaim her world—one wall at a time. The scent of mildew and old plaster that clung to The Old Crown Inn was slowly being replaced by the fresh promise of linen-white paint. But with every misplaced dab and errant streak, the inn seemed to resist her efforts, as if it were testing her resolve.

Her gaze shifted beyond the window, where the cove lay draped in a shawl of mist, the sea whispering secrets to the rugged cliffs. Here was the natural beauty she had sought—a stark contrast to the chaos she left behind in New York. Its wild tranquility was a balm, yet within these walls, that peace felt just out of reach.

CHAPTER SEVENTEEN

The afternoon sun filtered through the stained-glass windows of The Old Crown Inn, casting kaleidoscopic patterns on the faded wooden floor. Charlotte Moore stood behind the reception desk, her fingers mindlessly tracing the intricate carvings in the oak as she pondered a new color scheme for the lobby. A vibrant palette, perhaps, to breathe fresh life into the old bones of the manor house.

"Charlotte, darling," a voice as smooth as clotted cream interrupted her reverie. Isla Wagner appeared like a summer storm—sudden and impossible to ignore—with her windswept hair and an enigmatic smile that never quite reached her eyes.

"Can I help you with something, Isla?" Charlotte asked, forcing a polite smile while bracing herself against the brewing undercurrent.

"Actually, yes." Isla leaned against the counter, her gaze sharp and assessing. "I've been meaning to ask how you're finding little Chesham Cove. It's quite the change from bustling New York, isn't it?"

"Indeed, it is," Charlotte replied, noting the precision in Isla's inquiry, as if each word were a chess piece moved with intent. "But there's healing in the quiet, don't you find?"

"Of course," Isla purred, brushing a lock of hair behind her ear. She tilted her head slightly. Charlotte returned to the patterns of light on the floor, seeking solace in their transitory beauty. Yet, even as she contemplated the hues before her, her mind was awash with a different spectrum—shades of doubt and trust, intermingling. The faint buzz of Charlotte's phone broke through the tension, a lifeline thrown into turbulent waters. She glanced down to see Simon's name flashing on the screen, his call disrupting the rhythm of her heartbeat.

"Excuse me," she murmured, grasping the phone as if it were the hand of a rescuer pulling her from quicksand. She stepped around the corner into the quietude of the adjoining parlor, leaving Isla's calculating gaze behind. The intricate patterns of the carpet blurred beneath her feet, every fiber urging her to distance herself from the woman who held pieces of Simon's history she had yet to read.

"Hello?" Charlotte's voice was a hushed whisper, a contrast to the cacophony of emotions clashing within her.

"Hey, Charlotte," came Simon's warm timbre, a soothing balm to the sting of Isla's words. "Hope I'm not interrupting anything?"

"Ah, no, just... handling some inn business." She angled her body away from the foyer, pressing her free hand against the cool wall, craving its solidity against her palm. A lie so white it almost glistened in the dim room, but necessary.

"Good to hear." His laugh was a low rumble, the sound of earth settling after a quake. "We still on for later?"

"Of course," she confirmed, her voice steadying with each syllable. In the safety of his virtual embrace, the shadows cast by Isla's intentions began to dissipate.

"Can't wait." His words held a promise, an unspoken understanding of the refuge they found in one another's company.

"Me neither," Charlotte whispered, her heart finding its rhythm anew. Amidst the chaos Isla stirred, Simon was her constant, the lighthouse guiding her through fog-laden paths. "Listen, Charlotte," Simon's voice broke through the static of anticipation, "I'd rather not come back to the inn tonight while she's still around."

The words tumbled into the quiet space between them like stones into a still pond, and Charlotte felt the ripples cascade through her chest. She glanced up, catching Isla's reflection in the window pane – an oil painting of poise and curiosity, framed by the waning light.

"Let's go out instead," Simon suggested, a note of eagerness threading his words.

Charlotte exhaled slowly, her breath fogging the glass for a moment before dissolving into nothingness. "That sounds perfect," she replied, the corners of her mouth lifting in a small, secret smile.

"Great. I'll pick you up at seven?"

"Seven it is." She allowed herself to imagine the evening ahead, a canvas waiting to be colored with memories yet to be made.

"Look forward to it," Simon said, his warmth wrapping around her like a soft shawl on a cool evening.

"Me too," she whispered, sealing their plan with a promise woven from shared anticipation.

As she slipped the phone into her pocket, Charlotte turned to find Isla's gaze upon her, a blend of suspicion and curiosity etching her features. In that moment, Charlotte was acutely aware of the masquerade they both performed – one seeking solace, the other answers, both cloaked in polite indifference.

"Who was that?" Isla asked, tilting her head slightly to the side, her voice laced with feigned nonchalance.

"Old friend," Charlotte lied smoothly, feeling the weight of truth pressing against her conscience, urging her toward transparency. But this was not the time for candid revelations; the air was already thick with unsaid words and unasked questions.

"Must be nice, having friends nearby," Isla remarked, the edges of her lips curling with a hint of something unreadable.

"It is," Charlotte agreed, her response a life raft she clung to amidst the turbulent waters of Isla's probing.

"Anyway, I should get going," Isla announced abruptly, as if deciding there were no more secrets to unearth here.

Charlotte nodded, watching Isla's retreat with a sense of relief that left her knees weak. She was free, if only for the rest of the afternoon, to prepare for an evening with Simon where the only eyes that mattered were those filled with understanding and affection.

She stood rooted to the spot long after Isla's footsteps had faded away, her thoughts chasing each other in circles. Tonight, she would cling to the possibility of escape, to the hope of healing in Simon's presence, away from the inn's oppressive walls that seemed to hold Isla's shadow even in her absence.

Tonight would be about Simon and Charlotte, about the possibility of what could be built from the driftwood of past relationships. Charlotte clung to that thought, letting it guide her as she prepared to step out from the shadows of suspicion and into the light of healing.

CHAPTER EIGHTEEN

An hour later, Amelia stood in the foyer of the inn, staring blankly at the floor. Her shoulders were hunched, arms crossed tightly over her chest. She didn't look up when Charlotte entered from the sitting room, concern creasing her brow.

"Amelia?" Charlotte ventured softly.

A noncommittal grunt was the only response. Charlotte moved closer, reaching out to touch her daughter's arm.

"Sweetheart, what's wrong? Did something happen?"

Amelia flinched away from her mother's touch, taking a step back. "You know why I'm upset. And I don't want to talk about it."

Charlotte's heart ached at the coldness in Amelia's voice. "I'm sorry if I upset you, sweetie," Charlotte began gently. "I know my move and the divorce has been hard for you. If you need to talk, I'm here."

Amelia's shoulders tensed, but she remained silent. Charlotte waited, hoping her daughter would open up. The ticking of the antique grandfather clock in the hall seemed to grow louder in the heavy silence.

Finally, Amelia met her mother's anxious gaze. Charlotte held her breath, willing herself to be patient. She could see the hurt and confusion swirling in her daughter's eyes. Charlotte knew she had to handle things delicately. Rushing in or forcing the issue would only push her daughter farther away. For now, she'd give Amelia space. When she was ready to talk, Charlotte would be there to listen.

Amelia took a shuddering breath, her eyes flashing. "Why do you always have to be so smothering?" she burst out. "I'm not a little kid anymore, Mom. You don't need to monitor my every move."

Charlotte blinked in surprise at her daughter's sudden outburst. "Amelia, I'm not trying to smother you," she began gently. "And I wasn't watching you. I just want to make sure you're safe and happy."

"Yeah, right. Sure, you weren't. And that's exactly the problem!" Amelia exclaimed, throwing her hands up in frustration. "You don't trust me to take care of myself. You think I can't make good decisions."

111

She turned away, hugging herself tightly. Charlotte's heart ached at seeing her daughter so upset. She hesitated, then stepped closer, keeping her voice soft. "That's not true at all, sweetie. I know you're growing up. I'm just...adjusting to you having more independence."

Amelia whirled around, tears shimmering in her eyes. "I'm not a little girl anymore, Mom. I wish you could see that." Her voice broke on the last words.

Charlotte gently touched her daughter's shoulder. "I do see that, Amelia. And I'm so proud of the smart, capable young woman you're becoming." She smiled encouragingly. "We're still figuring things out, but I promise I'll try to give you more space. Just...talk to me too sometimes, okay?"

Amelia blinked rapidly, then nodded, a tentative smile crossing her face. "Okay, Mom." Charlotte pulled her into a warm hug, hoping this was a step toward understanding.

Amelia took a deep breath as she pulled back from the hug. Fiddling with the hem of her shirt, Amelia said, "About Nathan. We just...connected right away." She glanced up hesitantly. "I really like him, Mom."

"I see," Charlotte said slowly. She felt a pang of concern at this new information but tried not to let it show. "And how did you meet Nathan?"

"We ran into each other at the market in town. He was so easy to talk to, and he offered to show me around the area." A faint blush rose on Amelia's cheeks. "We've gone on walks along the coast and just talked for hours. He's so thoughtful and interesting."

Charlotte nodded, keeping her expression neutral. "He sounds lovely. But a long-distance relationship can be difficult, honey. I just want you to be realistic."

Amelia's face clouded at that. "I knew you'd react like this," she said, a defensive note creeping into her voice. "Why can't you just be happy for me?"

Charlotte held up a conciliatory hand. "I'm not saying you can't see him. Just...proceed with caution, okay?" She sighed. "My only concern is you getting hurt down the line."

Amelia folded her arms across her chest. "I don't need a lecture, Mom. I can handle this." Her jaw was set stubbornly as she met Charlotte's gaze.

Charlotte hesitated, then decided not to push further. "All right. I trust your judgment, Amelia." She managed a small smile. "I'm here if you ever want to talk more."

With a short nod, Amelia turned and walked out of the kitchen, leaving Charlotte pensive and hoping she'd made the right choice.

Charlotte watched Amelia disappear upstairs, her footsteps echoing down the old staircase. She sank into a chair at the kitchen table, shoulders slumped. Though she wanted to support her daughter's new relationship, Charlotte couldn't ignore the gnawing worry in her gut. Long-distance rarely worked out, especially for someone as young and inexperienced as Amelia. Charlotte knew firsthand how painful it was to give your heart to someone only to end up worlds apart.

She thought back to her early relationship with Daniel. It was exhilarating, romantic, magical—everything she'd dreamed love could be. But the inevitable strains took their toll. Charlotte didn't want Amelia to go through that heartache. But she also knew she had to let her daughter make her own choices. Pushing too hard would only drive Amelia further away.

She knew Amelia was mature for her age, but the thought of her only daughter so far away and emotionally invested in someone she barely knew still caused a knot in Charlotte's stomach. As a mother, her natural instinct was to protect Amelia, but she also had to let her spread her wings. It was a delicate balance, one Charlotte was still struggling to find.

When Amelia was ready, they would talk again. Until then, Charlotte would focus on creating a warm, welcoming home. And she would hope this new romance brought more happiness than heartbreak for her strong-willed, passionate daughter.

CHAPTER NINETEEN

The waves crashed against the shore, a soothing backdrop to Charlotte and Simon's seaside dinner. Candlelight flickered across their smiling faces as they chatted easily over wine and fresh seafood.

"It's so nice to finally relax together," Charlotte said, reaching across the table to clasp Simon's hand. His rough, calloused fingers enveloped her delicate ones.

"I've been looking forward to this all day," he replied. "Though I know you've had a lot on your mind lately." His hazel eyes searched hers knowingly.

Charlotte sighed. "I just can't stop thinking about Isla. Do you really think she's given up contacting you for good?"

Simon gently squeezed her hand. "Isla and I have been separated for years now. She knows there's no going back."

"I wish I could believe that," Charlotte said quietly, gazing out at the tumbling waves. Their rhythm soothed her fraying nerves.

"Hey." Simon tilted her chin back to meet his earnest eyes. "You have nothing to worry about with Isla. Or with us. Okay?"

Charlotte managed a small smile. "Okay," she acquiesced, trusting in his reassurance. For now, she would try to relax and enjoy their long-awaited evening together. Tomorrow's worries could wait.

Charlotte's smile faded as her thoughts turned inward.

"It's not just Isla," she admitted with a heavy sigh. "I feel like no one is taking my concerns seriously lately. Not about Isla, or my dad, or Amelia and this new boy, or the development plans for the coast..."

She trailed off, twisting her napkin in her hands. Simon leaned forward, his expression open and attentive.

"I wish someone would really listen, you know?" Charlotte continued. "Instead of brushing off my worries as paranoia or overreaction. I just want to protect the people and places I care about."

Simon nodded slowly. "I hear you. Your concerns are valid. Have you tried talking to Amelia again?"

At the mention of her daughter's name, Charlotte's face fell.

"Amelia's pulled away. She doesn't want my advice anymore." Charlotte's voice caught with emotion. "First Daniel, now Amelia...I feel so alone sometimes."

Simon grasped her hand once more, his thumb gently caressing her knuckles.

"You're not alone, Charlotte," he said firmly. "I know everything feels uncertain right now, but I'm here for you. We'll get through this together."

Charlotte met his earnest gaze, taking comfort in his steadfast presence. For now, she would try to push aside her worries and focus only on this moment, this meal, this man before her. The rest could come later.

Charlotte tried to focus on Simon and their romantic dinner, pushing her worries about Isla and Amelia from her mind. She took a sip of wine, letting the bouquet blossom on her tongue. As she set down her glass, movement from across the restaurant caught her eye.

Isla had just entered, weaving casually between the tables. Charlotte's grip on her fork tightened. What was Isla doing here? Tonight of all nights?

Charlotte watched warily as Isla made her way toward them, an innocent smile on her face. She came to a stop at their table.

"Simon! Fancy seeing you here," Isla said brightly. She turned to Charlotte. "And you must be...Charlotte, is it? I don't think we've met."

Charlotte's jaw tightened. Did Isla really expect her to believe she didn't know who she was?

Simon was frozen, his mouth open, seemingly unable to speak.

"Yes, I'm Charlotte," she replied evenly.

Isla beamed. "So lovely to meet you! I had no idea Simon was on a date tonight."

Charlotte saw right through her polite act. Isla knew exactly what she was doing. Still, Charlotte maintained her composure.

"Just having a nice dinner," she said. "Care to join us for a drink?"

She kept her tone light and friendly, not wanting to reveal her true suspicions in front of Simon. But internally, she vowed to stay alert. Isla was up to something, and Charlotte was determined to find out what. Charlotte studied Isla as she pulled up a chair and sat down.

"I'd love to join you both for a drink," Isla said cheerfully. She flagged down a waiter and ordered a glass of white wine.

Charlotte noticed how Isla's eyes darted between her and Simon, as if trying to assess their dynamic. Her questions seemed aimed at uncovering the depth of their relationship.

"So how did you two meet?" Isla asked with faux innocence.

Charlotte weighed her words carefully. "I'm new in town. I bought the Old Crown Inn."

Isla raised her eyebrows. "How lovely! And I imagine as a newcomer, you've gotten to know many of the locals." Her eyes flickered to Simon meaningfully.

Charlotte bristled at the implication but kept her tone even. "Yes, Simon's been very welcoming since I arrived."

"That's our Simon, always so friendly," Isla said with a tinkling laugh.

Simon seemed to choke—on air.

Charlotte nearly rolled her eyes. Did Isla think she was a fool? Her act may have worked on others, but Charlotte saw through the facade. She was determined not to let Isla get under her skin.

"Well, it's been so nice chatting with you both," Isla said after chugging her wine. "I'll let you get back to your evening."

Charlotte watched as Isla made her way across the restaurant, her unease growing. Though their conversation had been benign on the surface, everything from Isla's pointed questions to her overly friendly demeanor had set Charlotte on edge.

"How odd that she would play so fake, as though she didn't know who I was—I wonder why?" She turned back to Simon, who seemed shellshocked about the tension that had just played out. "That was...unexpected," Charlotte said, keeping her tone light despite her misgivings.

What was Isla after? Did she want Simon back? Or was she merely threatened by the idea of him moving on? Charlotte stared down at her half-eaten meal, appetite fading. They lapsed into silence.

"You've gotten quiet," Simon noted, his brow furrowing slightly.

"I'm just a bit distracted after...well, after our visitor."

Simon nodded, though Charlotte could tell he didn't fully grasp her unease. "I know Isla has a flair for drama," he said. "But try not to let it get to you. This is our night."

He smiled warmly, and Charlotte felt her anxiety loosen its grip slightly. She gave his hand a grateful squeeze. Whatever Isla's agenda, she wouldn't let it ruin this budding romance.

"You're right," she said, straightening up in her seat. "I won't give her power over this evening. Now, where were we?"

Though doubts still lingered in the shadowy corners of her mind, Charlotte resolved to push them aside. She wouldn't hand Isla the satisfaction of derailing this relationship before it could even begin.

Charlotte tried to refocus on her date with Simon, pushing aside her lingering concerns about Isla's sudden appearance. Sensing her shift in mood, Simon gently tilted Charlotte's chin up. "Stay with me tonight," he implored, his sea-blue eyes full of warmth.

Charlotte's breath caught in her throat. How she wanted to drown in those eyes, to be fully present in this moment with Simon.

"I'm here," she whispered. "I'm with you."

She pushed her worries aside and let herself get swept away by Simon's tide. This new beginning was too precious to lose to the undercurrents of the past.

CHAPTER TWENTY

"Good morning, Mr. Thompson," Charlotte greeted one of the guests, her voice a practiced melody of warm hospitality. She moved with purpose, the grace of an artist still evident in her gestures as she poured his coffee with steady hands. Despite the smile she offered, there was a tightness around her eyes that spoke volumes of the strain she felt.

"Thank you, Charlotte. Another lovely day at your inn," Mr. Thompson replied, oblivious to the silent battle being waged mere steps away from his breakfast table.

"Indeed it is," she said, her gaze drifting toward Isla, who sat poised and serene in the corner of the dining room. Charlotte's mind betrayed her composure, thoughts racing like brushstrokes on a chaotic canvas.

How does she manage to appear so collected? Charlotte's grip on the coffee pot tightened just enough for her knuckles to blanch.

"May I have some more tea, please?" Isla's request cut through the hum of the inn, her tone courteous yet distant. The words seemed to hang in the air, a challenge wrapped in the veneer of civility.

"Of course, Isla," Charlotte responded, ensuring her voice didn't waver. She poured the tea with equal parts precision and reluctance, keenly aware of Isla's gaze tracing her every move. *Just keep it together, Charlotte. This is your place, not hers.*

"Will Simon be joining us for breakfast?" Isla inquired, the question seemingly innocuous, but Charlotte felt the probe behind it, sharp and probing.

Charlotte hesitated, a momentary lapse that she quickly recovered from. "He mentioned he had an early meeting in town," she replied, forcing a neutral expression. *Why does she ask about Simon? What is she playing at?*

"Ah, I see." Isla's lips curved into a smile that didn't quite reach her eyes. "He always was dedicated."

Returning to the kitchen, Charlotte leaned against the cool stone of the sink, allowing herself the briefest respite. She closed her eyes, breathing deeply, drawing upon her reserves of patience. Yet even as she fortified her resolve, the image of Isla, calm and unassailable, lingered in her mind like a shadow refusing to fade with the rising sun.

The Crown Inn's morning calm shattered with the unmistakable sound of cascading water. A guest's sharp cry from the upper hallway yanked Charlotte from her reverie. Her heart pounded as she ascended the stairs, two steps at a time, to find a torrent spilling from beneath one of the bathroom doors.

"Out of the way, please!" Charlotte called out, pushing through the gathering crowd. She threw open the bathroom door to witness a geyser from what had once been an ornate antique faucet. Water sprayed across the Edwardian tiles, drenching the floral wallpaper and pooling around her feet.

"Good heavens, Charlotte, it's like the Thames in here!" exclaimed Mr. Barnes, a portly gentleman who held his wife's handbag overhead to protect it from the deluge.

"Mrs. Moore, do you need assistance?" another concerned guest offered, but Charlotte was already knee-deep in crisis mode.

"I'll handle this," she said with forced calm, though her mind raced with the cost of repairs, the damage to the inn's old bones, and the disruption to her guests' tranquility. *This is a disaster. An expensive, destructive nightmare.*

"Everyone, please return to your rooms or the dining area," she instructed, her voice betraying none of her internal panic. "We'll sort this out momentarily."

With a reluctant murmur, the guests dispersed, some whispering concerns, others shooting sympathetic glances. Charlotte knelt by the burst pipe, feeling the weight of the inn's fragility—and her own—in her hands.

"Charlotte, let me help," Isla's voice cut through the chaos, as calm as the eye of a storm.

"No, I've got it under control," Charlotte snapped, more harshly than intended. She didn't dare look up at Isla, couldn't risk revealing the chink in her armor. *Don't show weakness, not to her.* But the truth was, Charlotte felt anything but in control.

As she scrambled to turn off the main water valve, her thoughts were a whirlwind of invoices and dwindling savings. The inn was more than just a business; it was a symbol of her independence, her escape

119

from a life that no longer fit. And now, the specter of financial ruin loomed over her New York fairy tale turned English countryside saga.

She ignored the pulsing headache forming behind her eyes and the way her chest tightened with every breath. *Just keep swimming, even if the water's rising.* Her palms pressed hard against the damp tile, willing strength back into her frame. Charlotte Moore was not one to succumb to pressure; she'd built a life on resilience, on turning canvases of disarray into masterpieces. This inn, with its quirks and creaks, would not be her undoing.

"Charlotte," Isla's voice again, softer now. "Can I at least call the plumber?"

"Fine," Charlotte relented, her tone clipped. As Isla departed, Charlotte felt the sting of defeat. *She's everywhere, in everything. How am I supposed to build a new life with her ghost lingering in every corner?*

With a deep, steadying breath, she rose to her feet, flicking droplets from her blouse. The inn was her sanctuary—a legacy she'd fought for amidst the rubble of her former life. She wouldn't let it crumble, not due to water nor the waves of doubt crashing within.

Isla returned, waving her phone. "Hang in there, He's coming."

"Thanks. I will," Charlotte snapped.

"Resilient," Isla repeated, the word rolling off her tongue with ease, as if she were tasting its flavor. "An admirable trait. I'm sure it's what drew Simon to you."

The inn suddenly seemed to shrink around Charlotte, the walls pressing in with the weight of Isla's implications. A flush crept up her neck as she took a breath—a futile attempt to regain some semblance of order.

"Is that what this is about, Isla?" Charlotte couldn't help but confront the elephant in the room, her usual discretion eroding under the strain. "Are you here to remind me that you were here first? To mark your territory?"

"Charlotte—" Isla began, but Charlotte pressed on, her words tumbling out.

"Or maybe you're trying to win him back? Sabotage what he and I are building?" The accusations felt foreign on her lips, but once spoken, they hung there—real, tangible.

"Charlotte, I think you're misunderstanding my—"

"Am I?" The innkeeper's eyes blazed with a mix of defiance and vulnerability. "Because from where I'm standing, it seems pretty clear what your intentions are."

Isla's expression faltered for a moment, the smooth facade showing a crack. But Charlotte didn't wait for a response; she spun on her heel and walked away, leaving a trail of whispered doubts behind her.

In the solitude of her office, Charlotte sank into her chair, the confrontation replaying in her mind.

What have I done? The question gnawed at her, along with the fear that perhaps, in her quest for a fresh start by the sea, she had merely traded one set of troubles for another.

Isla's silhouette suddenly stood poised like an accusation in the office doorway. The old wooden floorboards seemed to groan under the weight of tension.

"Charlotte," Isla's voice broke the silence, her tone unexpectedly gentle, "do you really believe I could stop something that's meant to be?"

Her question was simple, yet it bore the gravity of a gavel. Charlotte hesitated, the taste of her own hurried accusations still bitter on her tongue. She turned slowly, meeting Isla's gaze—those familiar eyes now clouded with a hurt that mirrored her surprise.

"Because if Simon's heart is truly with me," Isla continued, her composure as unyielding as the coastal cliffs outside, "no force on earth could change his course. Not even your unfounded fears."

Charlotte wanted to retort, to unleash a storm of words that would sweep away Isla's calm, but she found herself mute, her thoughts swirling like leaves caught in an autumn gust. She watched Isla's slender fingers trace the edge of an antique side table, a touch as soft as a memory, and for a moment, Charlotte could almost believe in the other woman's innocence.

A door slammed somewhere upstairs, jolting them both.

"Simon will make his own choices," Isla said, her words laced with a finality that sent a shiver down Charlotte's spine. "Neither you nor I can sway him."

Charlotte's breath caught in her throat, the sharp sting of defeat mingling with the scent of beeswax polish and aging wood. She was suddenly acutely aware of every crack in the plaster, every frayed edge of carpet—the imperfections of The Crown Inn mirroring the cracks in her facade.

"Excuse me," she murmured, her voice barely above a whisper, as she stood and brushed past Isla. She needed to attend to the disaster unfolding around her to salvage what remained of her crumbling sanctuary.

But as she moved to the front porch to wait for the plumber, offering apologies and assurances with a smile that never quite reached her eyes, the seeds of doubt Isla had sown took root. Could she really protect her budding relationship with Simon? Was her fledgling start in Chesham Cove destined to wither under the shadow of Isla's enigmatic presence?

The questions haunted her, trailing her like shadows as she navigated the corridors of the inn. Each step felt heavier than the last, each forced greeting more hollow. The Crown Inn, once her beacon of hope, now seemed to close in around her, its walls echoing with the whispers of uncertainty and the specter of Isla's lingering influence. Her dream of a peaceful retreat by the sea had been tainted, the canvas of her new life splattered with unforeseen strife.

Yet, even as the shadows lengthened and the inn settled into a deceptive calm, Charlotte knew the turmoil within her was far from over. It had turned out that the plumbing fix had not been as disastrous as she had imagined—she chalked it up to stress and wallowed in some serious mortification at her overreaction—but with Isla's words etched into her conscience and the inn's troubles mounting, she was left to wonder whether her fresh start was just another illusion, as fragile and transient as sea foam upon the shore.

And now, the flooding—another layer of stress. Charlotte's footsteps were a silent surrender on the plush carpet of the upstairs hallway, carrying her away from Isla's piercing gaze. The confrontation had drained her of all pretense, leaving a raw and exposed core that throbbed with each beat of her heart. It had been more than she could give, more than she had anticipated. And Simon, with his easy laughter and tender gazes, had promised a future that now felt as unstable as the cliffside upon which the inn perched precariously.

"Can I even trust my own heart when it has led me astray before?" The vulnerability of the question made her shiver, despite the warmth of the late afternoon sun spilling across the desk. Each ray seemed to highlight the dust in the air, the imperfections, the reality that not all things could be mended.

"Maybe I'm not cut out for this," she whispered to the room, to the paintings, to herself. The idea of giving up clawed at her, but the exhaustion was overwhelming. She had leapt into this new beginning with a heart full of hope, only to find herself drowning in uncertainty.

"Where do I go from here?" Charlotte's gaze drifted to the window, to the horizon where the sky kissed the sea—a line that promised new beginnings yet remained untouchable. The Crown Inn, her supposed refuge, now felt like a ship taking on water, and she, without a lifeboat, was left to wonder if the shore of her dreams was ever truly within reach.

Charlotte exhaled deeply, her breath fogging the windowpane as she traced a mindless pattern on the glass. Outside, the relentless churn of the sea against the shore mirrored the turmoil in her chest. She watched seagulls wheeling carelessly above the waves, envying their freedom and simplicity.

"Think, Charlotte, think," she murmured to herself, her voice barely audible above the whistling wind that crept through the cracks of the aging inn.

"Fixing things... that's what you do." The words were an attempt at self-encouragement, but they hung heavy in the air, saturated with doubt. She turned away from the window, her gaze landing on the antique clock ticking methodically on the wall, indifferent to her plight.

"Can I afford the rest of the repairs if this is how things are going to keep going?" she whispered, her thoughts turning to the practicalities. "If this happens again—or worse!—insurance won't cover everything. And Isla..." Her fists clenched involuntarily at the thought of Simon's ex-wife, a storm cloud in human form, darkening the doorway of her new life.

"Every problem has a solution," she recited the mantra that had once given her strength. But solutions felt like distant stars, twinkling mockingly, out of reach. She needed a plan—a tangible string of actions that could weave the fraying edges of her world back together.

"Maybe a loan," she said, considering her options with a furrowed brow. "Or a crowdfunding campaign? 'Help save The Crown Inn'... No, too desperate." She shook her head, dismissing the thought as quickly as it had arrived. She didn't know how she would raise the funds if she continued to encounter house disasters, or how she would mend the rift with Isla, or if her relationship with Simon would survive the strain. The questions loomed like the evening fog rolling in from the sea, obscuring the path ahead.

"Tomorrow is another day," she whispered, her fingers lingering on the last word she'd written. The chapter closed with the scratch of the pen, leaving behind a sense of uncertainty and tension, like the charged air before a storm. How Charlotte would navigate the challenges ahead remained unseen, each possibility as unpredictable as the coastal tides.

She needed a walk to clear her head. She knew just the place to walk to.

CHAPTER TWENTY ONE

The waves gently lapped at Charlotte's bare feet as she trudged across the pristine beach, her shoulders slumped in defeat. The natural splendor of the coastline only mocked her now - the cries of the seagulls and the tang of salt in the air only served to deepen her despair.

In the distance, Windnell's ostentatious hotel gleamed atop the cliffs, its sleek glass and steel construction jarringly out of place against the rugged natural backdrop. Charlotte pictured the interior, all cold marble and chrome, devoid of any real warmth or character. Just thinking about it made her heart sink even lower.

Did she still have a chance to accept Windnell's offer? That would mean she would have to give up on her dreams for The Crown, but it would bring the financial security he promised. Already, the hotel's metallic footprint encroached further down the cliffs, its foundations burrowing into the earth. How long before the rest of the cove was swallowed up, transformed into something unrecognizable?

Turning away, Charlotte felt her resolve harden. She had come too far, sacrificed too much, to let her dreams be buried under glass and concrete. The Crown remained her last chance to build something real and lasting, a place where artistry and nature could thrive together.

Windnell wanted her to give up, to retreat back to New York in defeat. But the more he pushed, the more determined she became. She pictured Amelia's face, so full of joy and wonder when they first arrived. This place had seeped into their bones, become part of them. Charlotte refused to relinquish even an inch of it without a fight.

Picking up her pace, she strode purposefully across the sand. The wind whipped her hair as she walked, carrying the smell of salt and possibility. Charlotte breathed it in, letting it sweep away the last traces of doubt. She was ready now for whatever lay ahead. The Crown would survive, she vowed silently. Her legacy would not be glass and steel but wood and stone. Ancient, enduring, and full of heart.

Charlotte's phone buzzed in her pocket, jolting her from her thoughts. Pulling it out, she saw a text from Simon that simply read:

"Take a look at this!"

Below was a photo of a beautiful wooden sign, hand-carved with the name "Blue Horizon Fishing Charters" in an elegant script. Charlotte's breath caught in her throat. Charters? Her idea!

She typed back: "It's perfect! You did an amazing job. But, charters?"

Simon responded: "Couldn't have done it without your brilliant idea. Stay and play in Chesham Cove. This is just the beginning - with your talent, we can make The Crown a true landmark here."

Charlotte clutched the phone to her chest, feeling a swell of determination. Simon was right - this was just the start of what they could create together. She had so much more to offer this place if she just had the courage to keep chasing her dreams. Glancing back at the looming hotel behind her, Charlotte set her jaw. Windnell and his promises of wealth could not compete with the potential she held inside. She had come here to build something real, not get rich. It was time she started believing in herself again.

With a deep breath, Charlotte turned and continued down the beach. The wind lifted her spirits as she went, carrying her dreams - at last unfettered - toward the open sea.

Simon's next text popped up below the photo: "We got so many compliments on the sign this morning! Couldn't have done it without you. You really have a gift, Charlotte."

His words made her pulse quicken. She clutched the phone tighter, a renewed sense of determination welling up inside. If she could make this big of an impact on Simon's small fishing business, just imagine what she could do for The Crown if she put her whole heart into restoring it.

Charlotte turned away from the looming hotel behind her and continued down the beach, head held high. The sea breeze lifted her hair as the possibilities danced through her mind. She would not be swayed by Windnell and his promises of wealth - her dreams held something far more valuable. It was time she started believing in herself again.

Charlotte strode with purpose down the sandy shore, leaving Windnell's ostentatious hotel behind her. The cold wind whipped her hair as she walked, but she barely noticed. Her mind was focused, her resolve absolute.

She would not cave to Windnell's pressure or be tempted by his extravagant offers. The Crown was her dream, her fresh start, and she would see it through.

Charlotte pictured the old inn as she had first found it - the elegant bones peeking through years of neglect, the endless potential waiting to be uncovered. With her vision and Simon's support, she knew she could transform The Crown into the warm, welcoming place she had always imagined.

Windnell and his greedy plans would not destroy the tranquil beauty of this seaside village. She would fight to preserve the coastline with everything she had.

The setting sun cast a golden glow across the water as Charlotte left the hotel behind. She felt the lightness of freedom, of choosing her own path forward. The future lay ahead of her, bright with promise. With each step she took across the wet sand, Charlotte moved closer to embracing her true passion, realizing her creative vision, and breathing new life into The Crown.

Charlotte took a deep breath of the fresh, salty air as she walked further down the beach, away from the looming hotel. The wind whipped through her hair, tossing it back from her face. Looking out at the endless expanse of ocean, Charlotte felt a sense of peace settles over her.

This was why she had come here, why she had taken a leap of faith and bought The Crown Inn. This connection to nature, to the rhythms of the tides, to the openness and freedom of the seascape.

Behind her, Windnell's hotel rose like a monstrosity of glass and steel, its perfectly manicured grounds constraining the wild grasses and twisting the landscape into an artificial shape. Charlotte wanted no part of that world.

She belonged here, with the cry of the gulls and the hiss of waves rolling onto shore. She belonged with the rambling roses and weathered wood of The Crown Inn, nestled into the hills overlooking the sea.

The future held challenges, certainly - restoring an old building, fighting Windnell's development plans, proving herself as an innkeeper. But Charlotte felt only hope and anticipation. With each step, she embraced this new chapter of her life.

The sun dipped lower in the sky, casting crimson light across the clouds. Charlotte smiled, breathing deeply. She was ready for whatever lay ahead. The Crown awaited, filled with promise. But first, she needed to visit the harbor…

CHAPTER TWENTY TWO

The harbor, once neglected and dreary, was beginning to mirror the vibrancy of life Simon poured into it. Charlotte noticed new coats of paint on the weathered docks, the previously tangled nets now coiled with care, and the most recent addition: a small but charming bait shop that looked like it had sprung from the pages of a coastal fairytale. Progress hummed in the air, tangible in the form of restored fishing boats with their masts pointing proudly toward the heavens.

"Simon," Charlotte called out as she spotted him on the deck of his newly refurbished vessel, "the change is remarkable."

He turned, the corners of his eyes crinkling with a smile as he wiped his hands on a rag. "It's getting there. Slowly but surely," Simon replied, his voice carrying the same calm tide as the waters lapping against the hull.

"Your work... It's inspiring," she began, her words floating between them like the seagulls overhead. "I wanted to thank you. You've helped me see things differently—about the inn, about life here."

"Have I now?" Simon's chuckle was warm and genuine, a soothing sound amidst the creaks of the boats.

"Yes," Charlotte affirmed, gazing at the horizon where the sky met the sea in an endless embrace. She pondered how her view of the world had shifted since meeting Simon. The vastness before her no longer seemed daunting, but full of possibility. "You've shown me that starting over doesn't mean erasing the past—it means building upon it, learning to weave the old with the new."

"Sometimes all it takes is a fresh pair of eyes to remind us of what's possible," he said, leaning against the railing with an ease that spoke of years spent by the ocean.

"Or a kind heart willing to share its perspective," Charlotte added softly, her gratitude a gentle wave washing over her doubts. Simon's influence had been subtle yet profound. In his presence, Charlotte felt a sense of serenity that eluded her in the bustling streets of New York. Here, she could breathe, think, and create anew.

"Come on, let me show you what we've done below deck to support the tourist charters that you suggested." His invitation pulled her from her reverie, and she followed him down the narrow steps into the belly of the boat.

As they descended, Charlotte realized that the transformation of the harbor was not unlike her own journey. She, too, was being sanded down, repainted, and made ready to set sail on uncharted waters. Simon didn't just refurbish boats; he unwittingly restored hope to a wandering soul. And for that, Charlotte knew her gratitude ran as deep as the ocean itself.

In the subdued light of the cabin, Charlotte watched Simon as he gently traced his fingers over the smoothly varnished woodwork. The soft glow from the portholes cast a honeyed sheen on his face, revealing a man at peace with his craft.

"Simon," she began, her voice barely more than a whisper against the hum of the sea outside, "I can't thank you enough for... for everything."

He paused, his brow furrowing in genuine surprise. "For what? I've barely done anything, Charlotte." His hands stopped their motion, and he turned to face her, the shadow of confusion in his eyes.

"Sometimes it's not about doing, it's about being," she said, trying to articulate the sense of gratitude that swelled within her. "You've been an anchor in a time when I felt adrift."

"Charlotte," Simon chuckled softly, shaking his head. "All I did was show you around and talk boats. You're the one changing tides."

Her laugh joined his, light and unburdened. "Maybe so, but you reminded me that there's strength in still waters. That there's more than one way to navigate life's storms."

As Simon gave her a curious look, Charlotte's thoughts retreated inward. She had always prided herself on her independence, on her ability to steer her own course. But here, amidst the scent of salt and varnish, she confronted a truth she'd long avoided — her stubborn belief that she knew best often left little room for other perspectives. It was a realization that came in whispers, not shouts, much like the lapping waves against the hull.

She was learning to listen.

"Your outlook," she continued, turning her gaze toward the small window where the sea reflected the sky, "it's refreshing. It challenges me. The ex-wife detail. That's just frustrating."

"Happy to be of service," he replied, the bemusement clear in his tone. "Though I must admit, this is the first time I've been thanked for being... perplexing."

"Life's full of surprises," Charlotte mused, her smile lingering as she watched him resume his work.

It was strange, she reflected, how life's greatest lessons often arrived in unexpected packages — wrapped in the guise of a rugged fisherman with a talent for restoring boats and unwittingly, hearts. She had sought control in an uncontrollable world, yet now, standing beside Simon, she welcomed the unpredictable tides that had brought her here.

"Isn't it just?" Simon agreed, his hands once again moving with purpose over his labor of love.

Charlotte watched him work, each stroke of his hand a testament to his care and attention to detail. It was a dance of patience and precision, a balance she realized she needed in her own life.

"Indeed," she finally said, her voice steady as the horizon line. "And I'm starting to think I wouldn't have it any other way."

***

After her visit with Simon, Charlotte took a stroll into Chesham Cove's quaint embrace, the harbor a blend of nature's serenity and mankind's persistence. The sea breeze wove through her hair like an old friend's greeting, carrying the briny scent of adventure and the distant cry of gulls.

"Later," she whispered to herself, casting one last glance at Simon's project, where the hull of the boat gleamed under his meticulous care. The afternoon sun bathed the harbor in gold, but Charlotte knew there were other treasures she needed to uncover today. Her heart was set on mending bridges, not just admiring them from afar.

Determination settled over her like a shawl as she made her way along the cobblestone path that led toward the town's edge. Amelia would be there, wrapped up in the latest chapter of her young life. Charlotte's steps quickened with the thought, her mind abuzz with plans for their meeting. There was so much to say, so much to heal.

The path gave way to a lush meadow, where wildflowers nodded their colorful heads in time with the rhythm of the sea. Charlotte paused, a breath caught between hope and hesitation. This place, vibrant and untamed, reminded her of Amelia — full of life and uncharted potential. She could almost see her daughter's silhouette against the sky, her laughter weaving through the tall grasses.

"Amelia will understand," Charlotte murmured, more to herself than the open air, her hands unconsciously smoothing the fabric of her skirt. "She always does."

Taking a steadying breath, she continued, the soft earth beneath her feet grounding her resolve. Soon, the outline of the old oak tree came into view, its branches a testament to resilience. And there, as if part of the landscape itself, stood Amelia, her profile etched against the backdrop of the sprawling branches. The air was heavy with the scent of salt and seaweed as Charlotte approached the old oak, her heart drumming a complex rhythm against her ribs. She could see Amelia and the young man, Nathan, standing close together, their silhouettes carving out an intimate space within the wild embrace of nature. The sight brought a sudden tightness to Charlotte's chest, an echo of old fears mingling with hope.

"Amelia," she called gently, her voice carrying on the breeze.

Both heads turned, and the quiet bubble that had enveloped the pair seemed to pop, releasing a current of tension into the afternoon air. Charlotte watched Nathan's guarded stance, the way his arm fell from Amelia's shoulder, creating a careful distance between them.

"Mom?" Amelia's voice held a note of surprise as she turned, her expression a mixture of uncertainty and warmth.

Charlotte's heart swelled. "I was hoping we could talk," she said, her voice threading through the distance between them.

"Of course," Amelia replied, her gaze searching Charlotte's face. The air seemed charged with a thousand unsaid words, each waiting for its turn to bridge the gap.

As mother and daughter closed the space between them, Charlotte felt the weight of the past begin to lift, replaced by the lightness of possibility. And in that moment, amidst the wild beauty of the cove and the enduring strength of the old oak, Charlotte found the courage to embrace the unpredictable journey ahead.

"This is Nathan."

Charlotte nodded, already aware of the secret that wasn't quite a secret anymore. Her gaze lingered on Nathan, noticing the apprehension in his eyes, the set of his jaw. "I've heard a lot about you," she offered, hoping to ease the wariness that greeted her.

"Nice to meet you, Mrs. Moore," Nathan replied, his words polite but hesitant, like a man unsure if he was stepping onto solid ground or a hidden quagmire.

"Please, call me Charlotte," she insisted, her hand outstretched in peace. In that moment, she made a choice—the same way she chose bold colors on a blank canvas, daring to blend where others might separate.

"Actually, Nathan, I was wondering if you'd join us for dinner at The Crown Inn tonight?" Charlotte watched the surprise ripple across his face, a breaking wave that carried away some of the stiffness in his posture.

"Me? You want me to come to dinner?" Nathan's voice cracked slightly, betraying his astonishment.

"Yes," Charlotte affirmed, her smile genuine. "I think it's time we all sat down together, don't you?"

"Ah... Yeah, sure. Thank you." His acceptance came slowly, as if tasting the words before fully committing to them.

Amelia's hand found Charlotte's, a silent thank you woven into the gesture. Charlotte squeezed back, her own gratitude mirrored in the clasp. They shared a look, mother and daughter, recognizing this for what it was—a step toward mending, toward understanding.

Inside, Charlotte wrestled with her own insecurities. Had she done right by extending the olive branch? The artist within her knew that sometimes you had to mix unexpected hues to reveal the true depth of a painting, much like the unpredictable tides of relationships.

The tension that once knitted Charlotte's brow had eased, replaced by a soft openness as she turned to face her daughter.

"Amelia," she began, her voice carrying the weight of untold apologies, "I know I've been... difficult." Her gaze dropped to the sand, noting how the waves smoothed each grain in their retreat, much like time sought to heal old wounds.

Amelia's eyes, so much like her father's, held a storm of emotions. She stepped closer, the distance between them shrinking with each tentative movement. "Mom, it's okay. We've both been..."

"Stubborn?" Charlotte offered a wry smile, her hand reaching out to brush a strand of hair from Amelia's cheek. The gesture bridged years of silent misunderstandings, a simple touch conveying what words often failed to express.

"Stubborn," Amelia confirmed with a laugh that danced through the air, light and forgiving. "But you're here now, and that's what matters."

Charlotte nodded, the relief that flooded her was palpable, warming her from within. "I am here, and I love you more than the canvas loves the paint. You are my greatest creation, my most treasured piece," she said, her heart swelling with the truth of her words.

"Even when I act like a terrible diva?" Amelia teased, but her eyes shimmered with unshed tears.

"Especially then," Charlotte replied, pulling her daughter into an embrace that spoke volumes of the love that had never waned, even in the darkest of times.

"I can't believe I have to leave soon," Amelia sniffled.

Charlotte squeezed her tighter. "Me, either. I wish you would stay forever."

The moment lingered, two hearts syncing once again in the rhythm of shared forgiveness. As they parted, Amelia's hand clung to Charlotte's for a second longer, a silent promise that this time things would be different. Charlotte felt a sense of resolution blossoming within her. The journey ahead would be fraught with challenges, but the path felt clearer now, illuminated by the love she held for her daughter and the hope that, together, they could heal.

CHAPTER TWENTY THREE

Charlotte sat on the worn wooden porch of the inn, the breeze from the sea tousling her chestnut hair as she added delicate strokes of azure to the canvas before her. The cliffs and rolling waves took shape under her brush, capturing the wild beauty of the coastline.

A lone figure wandered along the cliff's edge, pausing as her gaze fell upon the painter. Intrigued, the woman drifted closer, her steps light across the swaying grass. Charlotte was lost in her work, blending the colors of sea and sky until they melted into one harmonious whole.

"What a beautiful scene," Isla said, her voice soft.

Charlotte started, looking up to find the woman's bright eyes fixed on her canvas. "Oh! Thank you," she replied, a faint blush rising in her cheeks.

"You've perfectly captured the mood here. I can almost hear the cry of the gulls and feel the salt spray." Isla tucked a strand of long, dark hair behind her ear. "You're very talented."

Charlotte studied the woman's delicate features and intelligent eyes. "Thank you for the lovely compliments," Charlotte said. "It's been wonderful discovering all the beauty here in Chesham Cove. Each day I find some new vista or hidden cove that simply begs to be painted."

Isla nodded, her gaze drifting back to the canvas. "You've certainly captured the spirit of this place. I can see why Simon is so taken with you."

Charlotte froze at the mention of his name. "You don't have to rub it in, that—?"

"We have a history together?" Isla's voice held a tinge of wistfulness.

Charlotte chose her next words carefully. "Simon is free to make his own choices now. I won't interfere in whatever relationship the two of you still share. You made that point clear, and I agree."

Isla looked surprised, then understanding crossed her face. "Simon—while I'll always care for him, our time has passed." She reached out and squeezed Charlotte's hand gently. "Don't let the past

135

hold you back from finding happiness. I can see that your heart is open and true. That's what Simon needs."

Charlotte took a deep breath as she processed Isla's words of encouragement. This was not at all how she expected their first meeting to unfold.

"Thank you," she said finally. "I know Simon still cares for you deeply, and I would never try to come between that."

Isla gave a sad smile. "We were just children when we wed. It was a foolish match, but we both felt trapped by our circumstances."

She turned her gaze out to the sea, the breeze catching strands of her chestnut hair. "I've come to make peace with the past and release Simon fully. We both deserve a second chance at real happiness. I'm sorry I was so difficult, I just—I was trying to see what you were made of. If you deserved him."

Reaching into her bag, she withdrew an envelope. "I was on my way to the harbor to file these - our signed divorce papers."

Charlotte's eyes widened in surprise. So it was true - Simon was finally free. Her heart swelled with hope and anticipation even as she tamped it down.

"That really is a beautiful painting," Isla said, her voice warm with admiration. "You've perfectly captured the mood here - the solitude, the whispering sea, the cliffs standing sentinel."

Charlotte flushed, unused to praise for her art. "Thank you. Painting is my refuge, it always has been."

"I can see why." Isla tilted her head.

"Of course." Charlotte set down her brush and gestured to the empty chair beside her.

Isla settled gracefully, hands folded in her lap. For a moment, neither woman spoke, listening to the cry of gulls and murmur of waves.

Finally Isla turned to Charlotte, hazel eyes meeting blue. "I know my coming here was unexpected, but I wanted to speak with you before...well, before things move forward with Simon."

Charlotte hesitated. "You don't owe me any explanation."

"No, but I want you to know - Simon is a good man. Perhaps I didn't appreciate that as I should have when we were young. He deserves to be cherished." Isla smiled ruefully. "And I can see now, you are the one to do that."

Charlotte flushed, moved by Isla's sincerity. "All I want is his happiness. I won't come between you, as I said."

Isla shook her head. "What we had was...different. More like companionship than real love." She gazed out at the sea. "I've spent so long trying to be the person everyone expected me to be. But here, I feel free - free to find myself again."

Charlotte nodded slowly, understanding dawning. "I feel that way too, since coming to Chesham Cove. Like I can breathe for the first time."

The two women shared a smile - a smile of shared experience and newfound kinship. The future stretched before them, uncertain but full of promise.

Charlotte took a deep breath, the sea air filling her lungs. "What will you do now?"

Isla tilted her head thoughtfully. "I don't know yet. But for the first time in a long while, I'm excited to find out."

She leaned down to pick up her bag. "I should be going. I have some papers to deliver."

Charlotte knew she meant the divorce papers for Simon. "I wish you all the best, truly. You deserve to find happiness, Isla."

"As do you." Isla squeezed her hand warmly. "Take care of that stubborn fisherman for me."

Charlotte laughed. "I'll do my best."

Isla walked down the rocky path toward town, her step lighter than before. At the edge of the cliff, she turned and waved.

Charlotte waved back, watching as Isla disappeared from view. She turned her gaze back to the endless ocean and smiled. The future was unwritten, but she knew one thing for certain - she had found her home here in Chesham Cove.

Mending her relationships with Simon and Amelia wouldn't happen overnight. The inn still needed extensive repairs. Her dad was still MIA. So many questions, and no easy answers. But for the first time in months, Charlotte felt a sense of hope blooming in her heart. Come what may, she knew she could weather any storm.

The cry of gulls drew Charlotte's gaze upward. The wheeling birds drifted on the ocean breezes, at home in their element. She envied their freedom, their lack of roots. But she had put down roots here now, deeper than she had realized. Chesham Cove was her home.

Charlotte turned back to her canvas, studying the half-finished seascape. There was still work to be done, but the foundations were strong. Mixing more paint on her palette, she smiled. Sometimes life was like painting - you simply had to trust the process.

With a light heart, she lifted her brush again, ready to embrace whatever the future held. The next chapter of her life was just beginning.

CHAPTER TWENTY FOUR

The sun sparkled on the calm blue sea as Charlotte stepped onto the deck of Simon's fishing boat. The salty breeze lifted her hair and filled her lungs with the invigorating scent of the ocean. As Simon unfurled the sails and the boat began to glide across the water, Charlotte felt a thrill of anticipation. They were sailing toward a small, uninhabited island just off the coast, a place she had heard about but never visited.

Charlotte leaned against the railing, eyes drinking in the beauty around her. Behind them, the picturesque village of Chesham Cove receded into the distance. Ahead, the island beckoned, its forested shores and rocky cliffs coming into sharper focus. Simon stood at the helm, strong and capable, guiding them steadily across the sun-sparkled sea.

Charlotte closed her eyes, letting the rhythm of the waves soothe her. How different this was from her life in New York. The bustle of the city, the sterile office, the stress and noise - it all seemed to melt away out here on the open water. She felt her shoulders relax and her mind quiet. A sense of peace settled over her.

"It's beautiful, isn't it?" Simon said, glancing back at her with an understanding smile.

"It's perfect," she replied. And it was. The island awaiting them, the man beside her, the new life she was building - this was exactly where she was meant to be.

Charlotte turned to Simon with a playful grin.

"So, are you going to impress me with your expert sailing skills, Captain?" she teased.

Simon chuckled, his eyes crinkling at the corners. "Well, I'll do my best, though I'm not sure my skills are that impressive."

"Oh, come on," Charlotte cajoled. "I'm sure you have all kinds of amazing stories from your years as a fisherman."

"Maybe one or two," Simon allowed modestly.

As they talked and laughed, Charlotte felt herself relaxing even more. Simon had a way of putting her at ease, of making her feel comfortable to just be herself. With him, she didn't have to try so hard or put on a facade.

As the island drew nearer, their words trailed off. They didn't need to speak anymore. A connection had been forged, a silent understanding. Charlotte reached for Simon's hand, interlacing her fingers with his. Eyes meeting, they exchanged a smile filled with promise. The future was theirs to explore together.

Simon expertly maneuvered the fishing boat into a small cove nestled along the island's rocky shoreline. Dropping anchor, he turned to Charlotte with a grin. "Well, here we are. Our own private paradise."

Charlotte's eyes widened as she took in the pristine beach framed by swaying palms and lush vegetation. The sand looked like powdered sugar, and the crystal blue water beckoned invitingly.

"It's breathtaking," she said. "I've never seen anywhere so beautiful and untouched."

Simon nodded, pride in his voice as he replied, "The islands around here are special. It feels like you've gone back in time."

Charlotte wasted no time kicking off her shoes and stepping onto the beach, the soft sand warm under her feet. Simon followed close behind as she wandered down to the shoreline, dipping her toes into the gentle surf.

Closing her eyes, she took a deep breath, filling her lungs with the scent of saltwater and tropical flowers. The sun washed over her skin, and for the first time in forever, her shoulders relaxed, tension melting away.

This was paradise alright. An escape from the chaos of her old life. A chance to heal and start anew. With Simon by her side, his solid presence grounding her, she felt she could do anything.

When she opened her eyes, he was watching her, an expression of understanding on his handsome face. "How about a swim?" he suggested.

Charlotte smiled and nodded, already pulling off her sundress. The water called to her, cool and inviting. With a laugh, she raced Simon to the surf, ready to savor this perfect day on their secret island. Charlotte surfaced from the refreshing ocean water, pushing her wet hair back from her face. She turned to see Simon emerging from the waves, rivulets streaming down his tanned, muscular arms.

They swam lazily in the shallows, bodies gliding effortlessly as fish darted between their legs. Charlotte marveled at the array of colors - teals, aquas, deep blues - all merging together in a watercolor painting.

When they finally retreated to the shore, Charlotte felt lighter. The ocean had washed away the last clinging stress, leaving her calm and deeply content. Simon unpacked a large picnic basket, spreading out a blanket on the sand. Charlotte's eyes widened at the feast - fresh baguettes, cheese, fruit, and a bottle of crisp white wine.

"This looks amazing," she said, settling down beside him.

"Only the best for you," he replied with a wink. "No Cornish Pasties, though. Sorry.,"

They ate slowly, savoring the food, trading stories, and laughing often. The wine soon had them both feeling pleasantly relaxed.

As the afternoon sun dipped lower in the sky, Charlotte leaned against Simon, head resting on his shoulder. His arm encircled her waist, holding her close.

She sighed in utter contentment. This small slice of paradise, here with this wonderful man - it was everything she had been missing. A chance to start over and follow her heart. She only hoped it would never end.

Charlotte closed her eyes, soaking in the warmth of the lowering sun on her face. She thought back to her life in New York - the sterile apartment, the endless appearances for Daniel's company, the fake-smiling cocktail parties, the growing distance between her and Daniel. It all seemed part of another lifetime now.

Here in Chesham Cove, she had found something real. Through hard work and determination, she was transforming the old inn into a welcoming home. She had made fast friends with the villagers, like Sally. She had reconnected with her art, the creative passion flowing freely once more.

And then there was Simon. Dear, steady, wonderful Simon, who had appeared just when she needed him most. With his patience and support, she was healing the scars of her failed marriage. He made her feel appreciated, cared for - loved. And she hoped she had helped him find closure with Isla.

She opened her eyes and looked up at him. "Thank you," she said softly.

He furrowed his brow. "For what?"

"For everything. For being there when I got here. For helping me with the inn. For..." she gestured vaguely, suddenly overcome with emotion.

He squeezed her shoulder. "You don't need to thank me. Just seeing you smile is thanks enough."

"I'm serious," she said, sitting up to face him. "I was so lost when I came here. But you helped me find my way again. I don't know what I would have done without you."

Simon caressed her cheek. "You're stronger than you know. But I'll always be here to remind you of that."

Charlotte blinked back, happy tears. The future was still uncertain, but she knew one thing for sure - she had found her home here in Simon's arms. Charlotte cherished these quiet moments with Simon, but a bittersweet feeling crept in as she glanced at her watch.

"Oh! Amelia's flight!"

She had lost track of time.

Charlotte and Simon made their way back to the pier, and she left him with a lingering kiss. She drove quickly to The Crown, and bustled upstairs to help her daughter finish packing. Amelia was folding clothes into her suitcase, a pensive look on her face.

"All set?" Charlotte asked gently.

Amelia nodded, then turned to face her mother, tears glistening in her eyes. "I don't want to go," she said in a small voice.

Charlotte enveloped her in a hug. "I know, sweetheart. I don't want you to either. But just think - one more semester, and you'll be done."

Amelia sniffed. "I'm really going to miss it here. I'm going to miss you."

"Oh, Amelia, I'll miss you too. So much." Charlotte stroked her hair. "But I'm also so proud of you. You're going to do such amazing things. Did you and Nathan have a good time this morning on your walk? You're keeping in touch?"

Amelia gave a watery smile. "Yes. Thanks, Mom."

They held each other tightly. Charlotte committed every detail to memory - her daughter's perfume, the texture of her hair, the shape of her shoulders.

Too soon, the taxi horn sounded from outside. Charlotte helped carry Amelia's bags out to the waiting car. She kissed her daughter's forehead.

"I love you. Call me when you land, okay?"

"I will. Love you too, Mom."

Charlotte watched the cab pull away, pride and sadness swirling inside her. But she knew Amelia was ready to fly. It was a new chapter for both of them. Charlotte lingered outside after the taxi disappeared from view, the bittersweet emotions still washing over her. But as she turned back to look at the inn, a feeling of peace settled in her heart.

The late afternoon sun cast a golden glow on the weathered stone and ivy-covered walls. Seagulls wheeled and called overhead, their cries echoing the endless rhythm of the waves. Charlotte breathed deeply, filling her lungs with the briny scent of the sea.

This was home now. The realization swept through her with certainty. She had found her place here in Chesham Cove, in the nurturing embrace of the village and the wild beauty of the coastline. Charlotte walked slowly up the path to the entrance of the inn, running her hand along the exterior wall. She could almost feel the steady heartbeat of the old building, its history and spirit woven into every stone.

She turned and looked out at the sea once more, the waters glittering like diamonds all the way to the horizon. Charlotte smiled, a sense of peace settling on her shoulders. She was exactly where she was meant to be.

Just then, she heard footsteps approaching behind her. Strong, familiar arms wrapped around her waist. Charlotte leaned back against Simon's broad chest with a contented sigh.

"I finished up work as fast as I could. How are you doing?" he asked gently.

"I'm okay," she said. "It's hard saying goodbye. But Amelia said she'd come back. In fact, she said she couldn't wait to come *home*."

Simon kissed the top of her head. "Good. I'm glad."

They stood quietly for a moment, watching the endless dance of the waves. Then Simon turned Charlotte in his arms until she was facing him. His hand came up to cup her cheek tenderly.

"You know, you've made this place feel like home for me too," he said, his voice husky with emotion. "You and that beautiful heart of yours."

Charlotte's eyes shimmered with tears. "Oh Simon..."

He lowered his head and captured her lips in a kiss both achingly sweet and simmering with passion. Charlotte melted against him, returning the kiss with all the love swelling inside her.

When they finally drew apart, Simon rested his forehead against hers. "I meant what I said," he murmured. "I want to build a life here with you."

Charlotte smiled up at him through happy tears. "I want that too," she whispered. "More than anything."

Simon's face lit up with joy. He pulled her close again, holding her in a warm embrace as the last light of day caressed the old inn behind them. Charlotte closed her eyes, safe and at peace in the arms of the man she loved.

This was home. A new chapter was beginning, and her heart was ready.

CHAPTER TWENTY FIVE

Charlotte's heels clicked against the cobblestone as she made her way into the heart of Chesham Cove. The salt-tinged, ozone-y breeze carried the sound of seagulls arguing over the morning's catch while shopkeepers swept their front stoops, chiming greetings to early customers. Charlotte inhaled deeply, the scent of freshly baked bread and blooming wildflowers mingling in the air—an olfactory testament to the harmonious blend of nature and community that had lured her across the Atlantic.

As she approached Sally's bakery, the warm glow from within spilled out onto the street through large, inviting windows. She paused for a moment, taking in the sight of golden loaves and iced pastries lined up like edible soldiers awaiting their march into the hands of eager patrons.

"Morning, Charlotte!" Sally called out as the bell above the door tinkled, announcing Charlotte's entrance. The baker's apron was dusted with flour, and her eyes crinkled with a smile that seemed to never quite leave her face.

"Good morning, Sally," Charlotte replied, returning the smile with one that reached all the way to her green eyes—a feature that mirrored the rolling hills surrounding the cove. "It smells divine in here, as always."

"Ah, that'll be the cinnamon twists. They're particularly feisty today." Sally winked, leaning on the counter. "How's the weather treating you? Looks like maybe some rain today."

"Actually, I find it rather refreshing," Charlotte mused, her gaze traveling over the assortments of confections. "There's something about the sea air that's invigorating. It makes me feel...alive. And it's perfect for a day spent painting by the cliffside."

"Speaking of which," Sally began, her voice lowering as if sharing a secret, though Charlotte knew it would be nothing more than benign local news, "have you heard about the flower festival next week?"

"Only every day since I arrived," Charlotte chuckled, her laughter mingling with the chime of the oven timer as Sally turned to retrieve another batch of what could only be scones. "It seems like the whole town is abuzz with preparations."

"Indeed, we are," Sally affirmed, placing the tray atop a wire rack. "And I dare say your contributions would make quite the splash. Your art—those landscapes you do—they capture the essence of Chesham Cove like no photograph ever could."

"Thank you, Sally. That means a great deal coming from you," Charlotte said, touched. Such words bolstered her confidence in the decision to preserve the unspoiled beauty of this place—a commitment etched into her very soul.

"Anyway, let me not keep you," Sally continued, packaging a few pastries. "You've probably got a day full of inspiration or renovation ahead of you."

"Indeed," Charlotte agreed, accepting the bag with a grateful nod.

"Charlotte," Sally said, her voice lowering conspiratorially as she leaned across the counter. The corners of her eyes crinkled with barely contained excitement. "Before you go, have you heard the latest whisperings?"

Charlotte, drawn by the intensity in Sally's gaze, rested her elbows on the cool marble, a smile playing on her lips. "Do tell."

"Word around town is that your father *might* be coming for a visit soon," Sally confided, her hands cupping her mouth as though shielding their conversation from the very walls that surrounded them.

A flicker of surprise crossed Charlotte's features, her eyebrows arching gracefully. Her father, the man who existed more in abstract memory than reality, seemed an unlikely visitor to this quaint seaside retreat—though he continued to be spotted around town frequently since the first mistaken sighting. Charlotte tilted her head, considering the possibility, but her heart remained guarded behind a fortress of skepticism.

"Really?" she mused, her tone laced with doubt. "And where did this intriguing piece of gossip originate?"

"From Mrs. Penworthy at the post office," Sally offered with an earnest nod, her voice dropping to a hush. "She claims to have seen an envelope with a postmark from Spain—and addressed in a hand she swears is identical to his."

Charlotte's mind wandered to the image of Mrs. Penworthy, peering over her spectacles with the shrewdness of a seasoned detective. She could picture the elderly postmistress examining the envelope with critical scrutiny reserved for foreign stamps and unfamiliar handwriting.

"Spain..." Charlotte echoed softly, her thoughts adrift. The country held no significance in her recollections of her father—a man whose affinity for distance and silence had been the only constants in her life.

"Could be nothing," Charlotte finally replied, her words punctuated by the gentle clink of porcelain as Sally set a coffee cup on a saucer. "Or perhaps just someone with similar penmanship."

Sally's expression deflated slightly, yet the twinkle in her eye remained undimmed by Charlotte's practical response. She knew the artist's inclination to draw conclusions only when the full picture was revealed.

"Maybe you're right," Sally conceded, the sound of her voice mingling with the hum of the oven. "But it's quite the talk of the town."

Charlotte gave a noncommittal shrug, her smile unwavering but touched with melancholy. She gazed out the bakery's window, where the world outside bustled with the simplicity of daily life. The thought of her estranged father wandering these cobbled streets seemed as incongruous as a shadow without form.

"Chesham Cove does love its stories," she remarked wistfully, her fingers tracing the delicate pattern etched into her coffee cup. "But some tales are better left untold."

Sally nodded sympathetically, her hand reaching out to rest briefly atop Charlotte's. Her voice lowered, losing a thread of its usual buoyancy, "I've heard something else... less savory than tart gossip about wandering patriarchs."

Charlotte felt a prickling sensation at the nape of her neck, a herald to unwanted news. She watched Sally's eyes, once dancing with shared secrets, now carrying a weightier message.

"Thomas Windnell is none too pleased with you, my dear." Sally's words were laced with concern, the lightness of their earlier conversation gone. "He's quite the influential one, isn't he? And you turning down his offer—it's made ripples."

A surge of defiance rose within Charlotte, her artist's fingers reflexively tightening around the porcelain handle of her coffee cup.

The smooth glaze beneath her touch was a stark contrast to the jagged edges of the predicament she now faced.

"Ripples can be weathered," Charlotte said, her tone even, though her heart beat an anxious rhythm against her ribs. Her gaze was steely, reflecting the determination that had driven her across an ocean to this quaint English village.

"Of course, they can. Still, he's not a man accustomed to hearing 'no'." Sally's brows knitted together in worry, her hands pausing in their task of tidying the counter.

"Thomas Windnell may have deep pockets and a London postcode," Charlotte replied, her voice resolute, "but I will not let him pave paradise to put up a parking lot—not on my watch."

Sally nodded, her admiration for Charlotte evident even as she pursed her lips, pondering the implications. "You're braver than most, Charlotte. Chesham Cove's lucky to have you."

"Bravery has nothing to do with it," Charlotte said, her mind alive with images of rolling hills and the rugged cliffs that cradled the town. She envisioned the cove as she first saw it, a palette of greens and blues that had captured her weary heart. She couldn't—she wouldn't—let Windnell's sterile vision consume the raw beauty that had become her refuge. "But thank you for the treat...and the warning, Sally," Charlotte said, offering a tight smile. Her pulse thrummed with an undercurrent of concern, but above it soared the clear note of defiance. "This town is more than just a dot on a developer's map. It's home."

"Good." Sally nodded, resolute. "We've seen tycoons like Windnell before. They come with their plans and their promises, but they don't understand the spirit of Chesham Cove. We're behind you, darling. All the way."

"Thank you, Sally. That means more than you know." With a heart fortified by solidarity, Charlotte pushed open the door, her departure marked by the tinkling chime that spoke of comings and goings, of endings and beginnings. Outside, the streets of Chesham Cove pulsed with life. Fishermen hawked the day's catch, their calls woven into the fabric of the cove's symphony. Shopkeepers swept their stoops, exchanging greetings and laughter with passersby. Children darted between stalls, their faces alight with the mischief of youth.

Charlotte paused, drinking in the tableau of daily life unfurling around her. The town was a living, breathing entity, its heartbeat synchronized with the ebb and flow of the tide. She felt herself buoyed by the collective strength of the villagers—their resilience an anchor amidst the tumult of her own upheaval.

"Windnell may have power and money, but he doesn't have this," she thought, her gaze tracing the outline of the horizon where sea met sky in an endless embrace. "He can't comprehend the bond that ties each of us to this place. It's not just land; it's a legacy."

"Let Windnell come," she whispered to the breeze, her words carrying out to the sea. "We will show him that some things—integrity, heritage, love—cannot be bought or bulldozed. They must be lived. They must be protected."

The conviction in her heart mirrored the indomitable spirit of Chesham Cove, and with a grateful exhale, Charlotte embraced the future, ready to stand with her community, whatever may come. Charlotte's heart, buoyed by the townsfolk's solidarity, beat a steady rhythm against the thrum of life around her. The murmurs of the sea were distant yet ever-present, like a backdrop to her every thought.

As she rounded the corner, she nearly missed the sight of the little jewelry store with its antiquated facade nestled between the vibrant greengrocer and the bustling juice shop. But it wasn't the quaint charm of the shop that made her pause—it was the figure of Simon Harris, framed within the display window's embrace.

He stood motionless, his rugged features softened by the glow of the store's warm light. His gaze was locked on something inside, and Charlotte could feel the intensity of his focus from where she stood, an invisible thread pulling at her curiosity.

"Simon?" she whispered under her breath, though he was clearly lost in his own world, unable to hear her gentle call.

She noticed the rise and fall of his broad shoulders as if he were taking measured breaths, perhaps steadying himself. The light played off his weathered jacket, hinting at days spent braving the winds atop his fishing fleet—days that sculpted him into the embodiment of Chesham Cove's unyielding spirit.

"Should I?" Charlotte wondered aloud, the words getting caught in the brisk air.

A knot of confusion tied itself in her stomach, and she took a step forward before halting, torn between the desire to know what captivated him and the respect for his private moment.

149

"Perhaps he's choosing a gift," she mused, tucking a stray lock of hair behind her ear, "or maybe he's reflecting on some memory." Charlotte's artist's mind painted scenarios, each brushstroke a question about the enigmatic man before her.

"Could be he's just admiring, like anyone would," she reasoned with herself, trying to shake the swell of intrigue that bubbled within her. Her fingers brushed against the cool glass of the display window, not quite touching it—as if the barrier wasn't just physical but symbolic of the distance she chose to maintain.

"Whatever it is," Charlotte finally conceded, "it's his moment." She gifted him one last glance, finding a strange solace in his silhouette—a contrast of strength and vulnerability that echoed her own journey. Charlotte's gaze lingered on Simon's back, a sturdy silhouette framed by the ornate jewelry store window. He seemed so intent, so absorbed in whatever treasure lay beyond her sight. A pang of longing nudged at her heartstrings.

"Let him have his secret," she whispered to herself, a half-smile playing on her lips as she imagined his eventual confessions over a cup of tea or during a windswept walk along the cliffs. She took a step back, the cobblestones beneath her boots grounding her decision.

And so, she turned and went on her way.

"Charlotte?" called out Mrs. Tibbs, the local florist, from across the street as she passed. Her voice was like a warm blanket, wrapping Charlotte in the familiar comfort of small-town life.

"Good morning, Mrs. Tibbs!" Charlotte called back, the exchange pulling her gently away from the world behind the glass pane of the jeweler's.

"Another beautiful day in Chesham Cove, isn't it?" Mrs. Tibbs remarked, her hands busy arranging daffodils that peeked out like suns from a sea of green.

"Indeed, it is," Charlotte replied, her eyes tracing the gentle sway of the flowers in the spring breeze. "We'll only get a few inches of rain—I heard there was a chance of sun sometime this week!"

The other woman's laughter followed as Charlotte continued down the street, her footsteps syncing with the rhythmic clanging of the boat masts in the harbor. Each clang sang of permanence and promise. As she walked, the scent of salt and seaweed blended with scents wafting from open windows, the quintessence of Chesham Cove filling her lungs.

"Charlotte, my dear," Mr. Kettleworth, the town's elder librarian, greeted her from his usual bench outside the library. "How's the inn coming along?"

"Piece by piece, Mr. Kettleworth. Like a mosaic," she said, picturing the Old Crown Inn's ongoing restoration. The metaphor wasn't lost on her—the rebuilding of the manor mirrored her own reconstruction, inside and out.

"Ah, but what a picture it will make once complete," he beamed, pride evident in his voice for the community's collective endeavor.

"Thank you," Charlotte smiled, her heart warmed by the thought of such unwavering support. "I couldn't do it without the help of this wonderful community."

"Remember, dear, the historical society wants the first tour," he said, tapping his cane lightly against the stone.

"You got it," she replied.

Taking a deep breath, Charlotte soaked in the camaraderie around her, the voices of Chesham Cove intertwining with the cry of seagulls above. She felt the strength of the cobbled streets beneath her feet, the resilience of the ocean waves in her veins, and the bountiful hope of the horizon within her grasp.

She turned toward the sea, its vast expanse a canvas for her future. The sun was blazing across the horizon, a masterpiece of nature's artistry. It was a scene begging to be captured on canvas, yet there was no rush. Charlotte knew the beauty of Chesham Cove was hers to embrace every day anew.

Charlotte stood at the edge of the water, her spirit dancing with the ebb and flow of tides that whispered of new beginnings. She held close the knowledge that, while the path ahead might curve unpredictably, the journey would be walked with the steadfast support of the community—and if her luck held, hand in hand with Simon Harris.

But she couldn't shake her curiosity over what Simon had been looking at in the shop, and she froze in her tracks when the thought occurred to her—Simon's divorce had just been finalized. Her heart hammered in her chest, and she turned on her heel to head back toward the jewelry store.

What if Simon had been looking at *engagement rings?*

NOW AVAILABLE!

A NEW LIFE
(Inn by the Sea—Book 4)

In this new romantic comedy series by #1 bestseller Fiona Grace, Charlotte Moore finds herself at a crossroads in life when her husband abruptly divorces her, leaving her with a failed marriage. Desperate for a fresh start, she makes a bold and impulsive decision to invest her last savings in a dilapidated inn on the picturesque seaside coast of the U.K. With the arrival of Charlotte's American relatives, family drama unfolds as Charlotte's long-anticipated meeting with her estranged father takes an unexpected turn. Despite the turmoil with her family, Charlotte can't help but fall faster for the man who won her heart, but she must make a decision about her uncertain future and the fate of her beloved inn.

"Wow, this book takes off & never stops! I couldn't put it down! Highly recommended for those who love a great mystery with twists, turns, romance, and a long lost family member! I am reading the next book right now!"
--Amazon reviewer (regarding *Murder in the Manor*)

"Wish all books were this good a mystery romance and love. Did not want to stop reading this book—loved it."
--Amazon reviewer (regarding *Murder in the Manor*)

A NEW LIFE is book #4 in a new romance series by #1 bestselling author Fiona Grace, whose books have received over 10,000 five-star reviews and ratings.

Upon her arrival to the seaside coast of England, Charlotte is immediately captivated by the enchanting surroundings and the crumbling historic house perched on the cliffs. With her artistic spirit, she can't resist the allure of the house's faded beauty and the promise of a new canvas for her life, and decides to take up painting again.

As her renovation begins, Charlotte stumbles upon a local man, a rugged fisherman, who at first seems like just another village face—but, beneath the surface, is a man with a vision.

In this heartwarming and inspiring romance series, Charlotte discovers the magic of daily life and the beauty of second chances, rekindling her dreams of purpose and romance in the charming, historic setting of the British coast.

A sweet romance series filled with twists at every turn, INN BY THE SEA will make you laugh and cry as it transports you to a magical place. A page-turner packed with jaw-dropping twists, impossible to put down, it will make you fall in love with romance all over again.

Future books in the series are also available!

"The story line wasn't just a who done it, but had a story about her life and romance, including village life. Very entertaining."
--Amazon reviewer (regarding *Murder in the Manor*)

"It has endearing and sometimes quirky characters, a plot that keeps you reading and the right amount of romance. I can't wait to start book two!"
--Amazon reviewer (regarding *Murder in the Manor*)

"What a great story of murder, romance, new beginnings, love, friend ships and a wonderful cascade of mystery."
--Amazon reviewer (regarding *Murder in the Manor*)

Fiona Grace

Fiona Grace is author of the LACEY DOYLE COZY MYSTERY series, comprising nine books; of the TUSCAN VINEYARD COZY MYSTERY series, comprising seven books; of the DUBIOUS WITCH COZY MYSTERY series, comprising three books; of the BEACHFRONT BAKERY COZY MYSTERY series, comprising six books; of the CATS AND DOGS COZY MYSTERY series, comprising nine books; of the ELIZA MONTAGU COZY MYSTERY series, comprising nine books (and counting); of the ENDLESS HARBOR ROMANTIC COMEDY series, comprising nine books (and counting); of the INN AT DUNE ISLAND ROMANTIC COMEDY series, comprising five books (and counting); of the INN BY THE SEA ROMANTIC COMEDY series, comprising five books (and counting); and of the MAID AND THE MANSION COZY MYSTERY series, comprising five books (and counting).

Fiona would love to hear from you, so please visit www.fionagraceauthor.com to receive free ebooks, hear the latest news, and stay in touch.

CALAMITY AT THE BALL (Book #3)
A SPEAKEASY DEMISE (Book #4)
A FLAPPER FATALITY (Book #5)
BUMPED BY A DAME (Book #6)
A DOLL'S DEBACLE (Book #7)
A FELLA'S RUIN (Book #8)
A GAL'S OFFING (Book #9)

LACEY DOYLE COZY MYSTERY
MURDER IN THE MANOR (Book#1)
DEATH AND A DOG (Book #2)
CRIME IN THE CAFE (Book #3)
VEXED ON A VISIT (Book #4)
KILLED WITH A KISS (Book #5)
PERISHED BY A PAINTING (Book #6)
SILENCED BY A SPELL (Book #7)
FRAMED BY A FORGERY (Book #8)
CATASTROPHE IN A CLOISTER (Book #9)

TUSCAN VINEYARD COZY MYSTERY
AGED FOR MURDER (Book #1)
AGED FOR DEATH (Book #2)
AGED FOR MAYHEM (Book #3)
AGED FOR SEDUCTION (Book #4)
AGED FOR VENGEANCE (Book #5)
AGED FOR ACRIMONY (Book #6)
AGED FOR MALICE (Book #7)

DUBIOUS WITCH COZY MYSTERY
SKEPTIC IN SALEM: AN EPISODE OF MURDER (Book #1)
SKEPTIC IN SALEM: AN EPISODE OF CRIME (Book #2)
SKEPTIC IN SALEM: AN EPISODE OF DEATH (Book #3)

BEACHFRONT BAKERY COZY MYSTERY
BEACHFRONT BAKERY: A KILLER CUPCAKE (Book #1)
BEACHFRONT BAKERY: A MURDEROUS MACARON (Book #2)
BEACHFRONT BAKERY: A PERILOUS CAKE POP (Book #3)
BEACHFRONT BAKERY: A DEADLY DANISH (Book #4)

BEACHFRONT BAKERY: A TREACHEROUS TART (Book #5)
BEACHFRONT BAKERY: A CALAMITOUS COOKIE (Book #6)

CATS AND DOGS COZY MYSTERY
A VILLA IN SICILY: OLIVE OIL AND MURDER (Book #1)
A VILLA IN SICILY: FIGS AND A CADAVER (Book #2)
A VILLA IN SICILY: VINO AND DEATH (Book #3)
A VILLA IN SICILY: CAPERS AND CALAMITY (Book #4)
A VILLA IN SICILY: ORANGE GROVES AND VENGEANCE
(Book #5)
A VILLA IN SICILY: CANNOLI AND A CASUALTY (Book #6)

Made in the USA
Las Vegas, NV
21 March 2024

87533304R00100